Creativ

Murder Mystery & Mayhem

Creative Quills
Writing Group

Murder, Mystery, & Mayhem

By Creative Quills

Creative Quills Publishing Group
El Reno, Oklahoma

ISBN: 978-0-9986436-9-4
Cover design: Andrea Foster
Thank you to Les McDermott for the great title!
Many thanks, also to our proofers:
Judy Bishop. Rosemarie Sabel Durgin, Julie Marquardt, and Jo Newton

To all those writers, perfectly lovely and normal people, who get a pen in hand — or a computer keyboard at their fingertips — and suddenly become dark and murderous scribes! 😊

TABLE OF CONTENTS

THE LATE SHOW

Bruce Baker

The station's jingle had barely finished when Steve's voice boomed out over the airwaves.

"Hope you are having a swinging time out there, Tulsa! This is Steve at Midnight, getting ready to play all the music you like to hear on the number one station in town, KMGT. As long as you're awake, I'll be taking your requests, and that means all night long, so give me a call on my hit line, PLA-MEEE."

Ever since the divorce, Steve Jamison had taken the midnight-to-six shift. The pay was better, and his deep voice seemed to resonate with the late-night audience. Not too excited, not too calm. Just right. Besides, there was no one at home, except every other weekend when his daughter came over from his ex-wife's place.

Laura didn't mind at all being alone at night, and he got to spend most of the day and early evening with her. Other than the short sleep time, it was a pretty sweet deal overall.

This Friday night started off like any other, just Steve and the equipment. No engineer or any other staff on the midnight-to-six run. Even the janitor was finished long before Steve showed up at eleven. That was when he got his playlist ready, so that when midnight hit, he could start spinning the songs that he knew from experience would draw in the late-night crowd.

Funny, he thought in passing, *I don't actually spin anything anymore, not since everything went digital.* That thought vanished as the calls started up, and between taking requests and modifying his call list with insertions from fans, the night began to fly by.

Somewhere around two am the phone rang.

"Steve at Midnight. What can I play for you?"

The words tripped automatically off his tongue as he worked the recording equipment.

"Steve?" A sultry female voice whispered hesitantly.

Damn, she sounds sexy, he thought. "That's me. Do you have a request?"

"Steve, I need you to play *Oh, How I Love You.* Can you do that for me?"

He knew the tune. The song had been incredibly popular with the teen crowd about four months ago but not so much with the older crowd. It still garnered tons of requests every night. Any thoughts about the sexiness of the caller vanished. He most likely could be her father!

"Is there something special about this song? A dedication?"

"Yeah Steve. You see, my boyfriend and I … well we had been together for about a year. Last week, out of the blue, he just dumped me. Just came out and said he didn't love me anymore. He told me that he had met someone else, and that it was special. Like what he and I had wasn't special? This song was our song. I hope he'll be listening tonight. I hope it reminds him of what he lost when he left me."

Steve had heard this sort of story far too often. Teenage love affairs were always complicated to the ones involved, especially the girls.

"No problem, I'll get that right up for you, miss…."

The line went dead.

Great, I don't even have a name to air with the call, he thought. The names along with the voices and dedications were what made the calls personal and not appear staged. A sexy voice like hers with a name would have been golden. "Oh well, it just wasn't in the cards tonight," he muttered under his breath.

It took him only a few clicks to locate the song in the digital library and only a few more to insert it into the playlist. He figured that the song would air in about twenty minutes. It paid to keep fans waiting…and listening.

About an hour and five callers later, the phone rang again.

"Steve?" It was the same voice, the same girl.

"Hi. Something else I can do for you?"

"No, I just wanted to thank you for playing our song."

"Did it help? Did he hear it? Did he call you?"

"No, but that's OK. I really didn't expect him to. I just wanted to make sure he heard it one last time."

Something in the way she said that last sentence caused Steve to catch his breath and his pulse to quicken. Something in her voice wasn't right. It was unnaturally calm for a distraught young woman, much calmer than the voice he had heard only a short time earlier. Steve confirmed that the digital recorder was getting all this and then continued with their conversation.

"Honey, are you all right?"

"I'm fine now. Thanks for asking. Not many people would care. He certainly didn't."

"What would make you say that?"

"I played it over my car radio right outside his window. He had to hear it. All the neighbors sure did. Lights came on all over the place, but he did nothing…nothing at all."

"Are you sure he was home?"

"Of course, he wasn't home, silly. He was over at *her* house."

"You played it outside her window?"

"Yeah. Poetic justice, right? The timing was perfect, too."

"Perfect, how?"

"Well, right after it finished playing, I let myself into her house through the back door. Broke the window and opened the lock. Easy-peasy. I used a rock covered in a rag to break the glass. They never heard a thing."

Steve didn't like the way this conversation was going, but he pushed her for more trying to keep her on the line, again making sure it was all recorded.

"What happened then?"

"Well, they were making a lot of noise up there, if you know what I mean, so I took the opportunity to wander over to the kitchen stove. It was one of those older ones without electric ignition, so I blew out the pilot lights, and then turned on the gas full blast."

"You turned on the gas and then left them to suffocate?!" He had to get an address and then call the police.

"No! That would be way too good for them. I just left a lit candle by the doorsill as I left and stuck the rag into the hole in the glass, so the gas couldn't escape."

Mentally, Steve tried to figure how much time

the couple had before the gas built up to a critical point, but before he could even hazard a guess, almost as if on cue, a thunderous explosion pulsed over the phone line, driving his recorder into the red with its intensity. When it passed, it was replaced by the girl's shrill laugh.

"Oooh. That was so much more impressive than I thought it would be." The excitement in her voice was electric.

Steve was thunderstruck. Had he just witnessed the murder of two people over the phone? He only had the one phone/land line and felt that it was more important to keep the caller on the line than hang up. From the sound of the explosion, the police and fire departments would be descending on the area long before he could get a call through on his cell. He took a moment to regain his composure, before finally returning his attention to her call.

"Honey, are you still there?"

"Of course! Where else would I be? This is fantastic!"

"What was that noise?"

Her reply surged with the adrenalin in her blood. "That was the house exploding. It was just like in the movies. One second, nothing. The next, BOOM! There is flaming wood going everywhere and a big hole where the house was!"

Steve could hear distant sirens approaching over the phone. He had to give them a chance to catch her there.

"I just had a thought. You know my name, but I don't have a clue about yours."

"Yeah, right. It's Linda."

Steve was about to push for a last name when her voice interrupted him.

"Steve, are you still there?"

"Still here. Not sure what to say to someone who just blew up a house."

"It had to happen. They had to pay for what they did to me."

"Linda, you do realize that you killed them, right? In cold blood?"

"What else could I do? He just threw me away for that little piece of trash, and then flaunted her in front of me. I couldn't let that go, could I? There has to be some kind of justice for the pain they put me through."

Her voice was racing now. He had to settle her down, keep her there until the police arrived.

"Honey, calm yourself. I understand. It's all going to be OK. Can I ask you a question, though?"

Her voice seemed steadier, less frantic when she replied, "Sure."

"Why me, Linda? Why did you call my show?"

Steve wasn't pretending here. He really wanted to know.

"I listen to your show every night. I feel like you get me. Besides, I wanted you to hear it from me, not some person who didn't matter. It needed to come from me."

"I'm afraid I don't understand…"

Her voice became impatient. "Steve. Your daughter was the slut my boyfriend left me for. Your pretty, blond, perfect daughter. They were doing it in your house, so it was only right that I used your house to kill them. Makes perfect sense, right?"

"What?!" *His daughter dead? His house destroyed?*

Steve suddenly found it hard to breathe as the depth of what he had witnessed settled in. He flailed at his chest as if somehow his near useless arms could force his lungs to work again. Then his vision blurred, and shooting pains ran down his arm. As he crumpled to the floor of the studio, the phone spilled out to his side. His eyes fluttered, then closed one last time as the voice on the phone continued.

"Steve, are you still there? You know, I would have called you anyway. You're the best. I love your show."

A DARKNESS RISING

Judy Winchester Beitia

I walk into my apartment and set down my keys like normal.

Suddenly, I find myself waking up on the floor. The silence around me is deafening, and all I can see is darkness. Trying to pick myself up, I realize I can't move. I reach out, despite my groggy mind, to wiggle my fingers and toes, and I'm met with immense heaviness.

Oh, no! I must have fallen, and I'm now paralyzed! How could that even be possible? I can still feel my body, I just can't move.

As I take in a breath, my nose and lungs sting with the stench of sulfur and putrid rotting flesh. My mind starts to race with scenarios fit for "Dateline," as my heart rate increases. I try to scream for help. Nothing. I feel like I'm lying on a cold metal slab of some sort.

Oh, Jesus, I'm dead and in the morgue.

I take another deep breath, trying to calm myself, but the stench is still heavy in the air. I start to feel nausea roll over my body, making my stomach twist. I can't be dead if I can still breathe.

I slowly open my eyes to take in my surroundings, but everything is a bit hazy. The room is darker now, so some time has passed since I got home.

As my eyes start to regain focus, I let my gaze wash over the room. Its dingy gray walls look like an abandoned house, with cracks running from halfway across the ceiling, down the wall to my right, then down to the floor. I half expect the smell of mildew, due to what looks like a huge water stain in one of the corners that creeps halfway down the wall.

My heart starts to pound so loud, I can hear it in my ears. That is not water; it is blood. I try to thrash around to get up but still nothing. Then I notice a dim glow from the area just out of sight above my head. I look at my body the best that I can, and I'm not being held down by anything!

God, that smell is getting stronger. I feel bile rise up through my throat, threatening to choke me to death, as I can't move.

Just then, the light grows dimmer and starts to flicker, as if someone is in the room with me. I try to plead for help but still nothing. The heavy throbbing of my heart in my ears gives way to a high-pitched ringing in my ears as my hearing is starting to return. The ringing fades and is replaced with muffled screams echoing in the room and the blinking of the light as it flickers.

Then, without warning, I see movement creeping along the ceiling. There is a child-like shape, but I can't make out what it is. As it slithers along the ceiling from above my head to across the room, it pools into a gelatinous blob. I close my eyes with hopes that this is a dream and that I will wake up.

My eyes shoot open when I hear something dripping to the floor. A slurpee-wet glop falls, hitting the floor with a plop, and sizzles as if the floor is a blazing hot skillet. Each drip that falls looks like black tar oozing down to the floor, congealing back into the childlike form at the end of the table.

My heart threatens to burst out of my chest as this creature moves in complete silence and gets larger, as if it is feeding off of my fear. The blob is now the size of a basketball player. I can feel sweat bead on my hands as terror continues to wash over me. Adrenaline is running through my veins, feeling like enough to put down an African elephant. The creature starts to hover and float above me.

I look into what should be its eyes, and I am met with nothing but a black void. It looks as if someone has shrink-wrapped a head with black patent leather, leaving nothing but sunken eyes that still seem to burrow through my soul.

Its darkness is like nothing I have ever seen

before. It seems to be sucking all of the light and energy from the room, leaving nothing but deep sorrow lingering in the air. Suddenly, its long arm reaches out to my chest, and I can feel it pulling at me with its icy grip, followed by a burning stinging sensation.

NO!

I'm being sliced open from my neck down to my groin, and it is pulling out and tugging on my insides. Tears fall from the corners of my eyes. The pain is overwhelming, and there is nothing I can do to stop the horrific scene unfolding in front of me.

I look down to see if I'm bleeding out and how much longer I have to endure this torturous hell. Nothing. My body is still just lying on the table as it was just a moment before, but now there is light being pulled from my core and sucked into the creature above me. The screeching that emanates from the creature as it feeds on my soul has started to drown out the other echoing screams. Everything starts to get fuzzy and fade. This must be what death feels like.

"If you are going to survive this, you must do as I say." A man's voice echoes in my brain.

I must be dying. I'm hearing voices.

"You must recite this prayer and make this sign." A symbol flashes in my mind, along with some weird words.

"You have to do it now! You don't have much time left."

My attention shifts back to my body, and I feel as if my intestines are being pulled inch by inch out of my body. A new pain invades my body, tingling, like a thousand little needles pricking my tongue, like when your arm wakes up from lack of blood circulation, only a hundred times worse. I have to try something to escape this hell, but all I have is languid tongue movement.

I recite the words in my head, hoping I'm saying it right. I notice the creature shudder; then I lift my throbbing tongue to the roof of my mouth and trace the symbol that was flashed in my mind a few seconds before. The pain stops instantly!

The blob has stopped pulling the light from me and is now shrieking and howling at me. It juts backwards, as if repulsed by me. I make the sign again. Now it's morphed into a huge glob suspended mid-air, rolling and twisting violently like ribbons of smoke, whipping out, then back in on itself.

I make the sign again. With a bright flash, I'm back in my apartment, sprawled on the living room floor.

What the hell is wrong with me? I moan, while reaching down to feel my stomach. I am still intact.

With a throbbing headache, I get up, and that smell is still stuck in my nose, not nearly as strong as before. It slowly dissipates, and I am left with the normal cinnamon apple smell of my apartment.

After a quick shower to wash away the funk, I head out to work.

I bob and weave my way over to the new customer, seated by the large picture window overlooking the street. I look him over, feeling my cheeks flush pink.

He has to be a model or something. Even though he is sitting looking out the window, you can tell he has a muscular build by the way his sports jacket is tightly clinging to his biceps while he rests his hands on the table. His dark brown hair is pulled back into a small messy bun at the back of his head, with just a few stray hairs falling down the side of his face. His jawline is strong and square, peppered with stubble, like he hasn't shaved in a week. His jeans are faded and have a small rip. They look to be designer, of course; they would hug in all the right places.

"Hi, welcome to Joe's Cafe. I'm Anna. Can I take your order?" I ask.

He turns and looks at me. His eyes seem to burrow into my soul. They are a dark brown, almost black, dark enough you could fall in and get lost and never be found again. "Yes," the man replies. My heart jumps up into my thoughts, with the realization that his voice is the same from my dream.

"Coffee, black, no sugar."

"Coming right up." I spin around and briskly walk back to the counter, trying not to trip over myself and the exiting lunch crowd. I catch myself, just staring at him from the coffee station.

Come on Anna, pick your damn jaw up off the floor, and take that hunk of a man his coffee.

Just then, a smirking smile creeps onto his face.

Oh, dear god, I hope I didn't say that out loud.

"Here's your coffee, sir. Can I get you a burger or anything else?"

Like me?! Ugh! I've got to get a grip on myself.

"No, just the coffee for now is fine."

To keep my mind from further exploring the gutter, I make myself busy with cleaning up after the last customer that left. I may be paranoid, but just like the rabbit being stalked, about to become a hungry wolf's dinner, I feel someone staring at me. With the table cleared, I head over to check up on Mr. Mysterious.

"Anastasia."

I whip around, almost giving myself whiplash, making me feel a bit woozy from the sudden movement, to see who has called my name. Not seeing anyone else in the dining room, I look over at the man by the window. He is the only customer left. When his eyes meet mine, I hear his voice again.

"We need to talk"

My heart begins racing as I realize his mouth has never moved. Now on the verge of hyperventilating, darkness overtakes me.

How did I get here? I think, coming to the realization I am at home in bed.

"I brought you here so we can talk alone," a voice calls from across the room. I realize that Mr. Mysterious from the cafe is in my room. I must have hit my head hard, and I'm hallucinating.

"Who are you?" I say, while sitting up to face him.

"My name is Michael," he replies.

"What's going on?"

"You have been chosen to help battle the darkness that threatened to take you over this morning."

"No, no, no! This can't be happening! That was just a dream. None of it was real!" My voice has become a bit shaky with the realization of what he has just said.

"It was real. You were able to save yourself from the darkness with my help. We have been looking for you for some time, and I'm here to start your training as part of the elite guard."

"This is crazy," I say, while flailing my arms, gesturing to everything. "I'm just a waitress, not a warrior!" I get up to leave my room. When I open the door, everything changes. We are surrounded by a room of white light that goes on forever in all directions.

My thoughts frantically swirl around in my head, trying to get a grip on what is happening.

This is in my head. I'm dreaming! I must be!

I pinch myself. Okay, that hurts, but so did the other dream.

Before the man can say anything else, I decide that this is one of those lucid dreams, and I am going to make the best of the situation before I wake up.

With determination in each stride, I approach him and wrap my arms around his neck, inhaling his scent. He is earthy with hints of sandalwood and vanilla.

His eyes widen at the sudden contact. Then I lean up and kiss him. His lips are softer than I expect. After a brief moment, he reciprocates the kiss--soft at first, then more firm. A feeling of hunger and urgency has seemed to engulf him. Before desire fully engulfs us, he breaks away from me, and we are back in my room staring at each other, both breathing heavily from the kiss that said more than any words could.

"That was your training ground for your mental shield training," Michael says as he straightens out his shirt and jacket.

My face begins to flush bright red as I realize I wasn't sleeping. I just kissed a total stranger like it was the end of the world.

"We will be meeting there regularly, but I think it would be best to start on your battle training first."

My insides start to twist with the realization that I'm going to battle darkness.

Our training has been rigorous for weeks. Every day is the same. I go to work to keep up appearances, then hurry off to the clearing just outside of town to spend several hours mastering my fighting skills. Then, when I am thoroughly exhausted, we set to work on my mental space and make sure I am staying grounded and keeping my shields up effectively, keeping Michael either on the outside of the space or keeping him trapped in.

Once all the training is done, we head off for dinner; then he leaves. But the last couple of days, he has been lingering a little longer each day after we would normally say our goodbyes. Tonight, I decide I want to walk through the park that is in-between where we have just finished our meal and my apartment.

"You want company on your walk? Michael asks.

"Sure, why not?"

While walking through the park, I realize that he keeps getting closer and closer, till our hands brush up against each other. Electricity courses through my body at the touch, and I feel a warmth take over me, knowing that my face has flushed pink, for sure.

Just then. without warning, I am up against a tree, just off the path, out of the way of prying eyes.

"How are you doing this to me?"

"What are you talking about? We were walking. Now I'm backed up to this tree. I should be the one asking questions."

To my astonishment, he leans closer to me and kisses me softly and lingers longer than before, making my head swim with emotions that I thought I had shoved deep down, never to see the light of day.

As he moves back just enough to catch his breath from the intensity that has just taken place, my ears are filled with a high-pitched ringing, threatening to crack my skull in two. And like a puppet on a pull string, Michael goes flying backward and is trashed into a tree and is now lying crumpled on the ground, not moving.

The battle has begun.

THE LEGEND OF WINK SIZEMORE

Judy K. Bishop

Ole Wink became a legend when he was only a boy. His story has been passed down through generations of family and neighbors, far and wide. He grew up in poverty in Appalachia, in the Great Smoky Mountains.

He was the youngest of nine children. His daddy worked in the coal mines. Mama, of course, worked in the home, raising the kids and running their four-acre farm in Rough Creek Holler. They were better off than a lot of their neighbors and kin folk. They had a mule and a cow, as well as chickens.

Mama Bessy had inherited the farm from her folks. Since Wink's daddy was away in the mines most of the time, Mama Bessy and the kids survived the best they could. As each child got older, they took on more responsibility of the farm and daily living.

Wink's real name was Chester. He got the name Wink, because his right eyelid drooped a little, like he was about to wink. The kids made fun of him, giving him the nickname, "Wink", which stuck all his life. Being the youngest, he got away with more mischief. With nine kids to wrangle, Mama Bessy didn't have much time or energy for a lot of discipline.

When Wink was around nine years old, he and a couple of his friends, Jake and Henry, were out exploring one day. There were abandoned coal mines in the area, with "No Trespassing" signs posted, but that only enticed the boys to enter, as they weren't thinking about any danger—or even any wild animals that might be lurking inside.

On this particular day, after finishing his chores, Wink met up with Jake and Henry for some exploring of an old mine they'd recently discovered. Jake was hesitant to enter this one. It wasn't the first time they had explored abandoned mines, but for some reason, Jake had a bad feeling about this particular one.

"Guys, I got a bad feelin' about this place. Let's go somewhere else."

Wink, not one to be dissuaded easily, said, "What are yer afraid of Jake? The boogy man might be in there?"

Laughing, Henry joined in, clucking like a chicken. "Your chicken wings are showing, Jake."

Wink and Henry headed toward the entrance. Jake followed, not wanting to be left behind or being called chicken by others at school. They had each brought a flashlight, knowing it would be dark inside Finding nothing unusual they hadn't seen before in an abandoned mine, they only spent about half an hour exploring before deciding to leave and move on to something more exciting.

As they walked out, Henry stumbled over something and let out a yelp. "Dag nabbit, I hurt my toe."

"Oh, don't be a baby," chided Jake. "Come on, you just tripped over a rock, you'll live."

Henry aimed his flashlight down at the ground, expecting to see a rock that had tripped him up.

"Wait, guys, come here, look! It weren't no rock I tripped over. It's some kinda leather bag."

Wink and Jake went back to where Henry was shining his light, to see this bag for themselves. Sure enough, it was a leather bag. The three of them stared at the bag for a few minutes before anyone spoke.

Finally, Jake said, "Well, let's open it and see if anything's inside."

Henry spoke up. "Since I found it I'll open it."

Henry slowly opened the bag, and then there was silence as all three boys stood there in disbelief and amazement.

"Do ya think it's real?" asked Wink.

"Looks real to me," said Henry.

"Yeah, to me, too," chimed in Jake.

Slowly, they bent down to get a closer look. The bag was full of money! All three boys were speechless. Finally, Wink said, "What do you think we should do?"

"We could run off and be rich and do whatever we want," said Jake.

Henry spoke up. "Don't be silly. We're just kids. We can't run off anywhere. I guess we have to go home and tell our folks. Then, they can decide what to do."

"Let's take it with us," suggested Jake.

"Yeah," both Henry and Wink said at the same time.

As they reached the entrance, bag of money in hand, they heard a deep voice.

"What you boys doin' with that there bag? Where you think yer goin?"

All three froze in fear, stopping in their tracks, coming face to face with a tall, scruffy looking man.

"Give me that bag! It's mine! And then you young-uns, scat, and don't tell nobody 'bout what you found."

Jake and Henry began to run, but Wink stayed put, still holding the bag.

"You don't scare me none, mister. It's our bag. We found it," Wink stated firmly.

Henry and Jake stopped and began screaming at Wink. "Come on, Wink! We gotta get outa' here!"

"I'm not handin' nothin' over to this scum bag. We found it. It's rightfully ours." Wink stood his ground, glaring at the man.

The stranger was glaring back and closed his fists in anger. "G'mme that bag or you'll be sorry."

Then Wink exploded into an all-out rage. The boys and the man watched in disbelief as Wink puffed up, grew six inches taller, and his eyes lit up like the eyes of a monster. Wink said in a low, calm tone that sounded like some kind of demon, "I'm tellin' you, mister, you git. We're taking this bag."

The man laughed and lurched toward Wink. Before he could grab him, Wink turned into something like a wild grizzly bear. Hair grew all over his body as he attacked the man, pushing him to the ground, while biting and clawing him mercilessly.

The man began screaming in pain, begging Wink to get off him, blood spewing from his wounds, but Wink didn't let up.

"Wink, stop! Yer gonna kill him," screamed the boys.

Finally, after what seemed like an eternity, the man was able to free himself from Wink and ran off, without the bag.

Jake and Henry stood in disbelief of the horror they had just witnessed. Right before their eyes, as quickly as Wink had transformed into this wild animal, he shrunk back down to his normal size and turned back into the boy they knew as Wink.

Wink looked confused, "What just happened?"

"You turned into some kind of beast and attacked that man and almost killed him," stated Henry.

They all sat silent for a few minutes. Finally, Wink spoke up, "Let's go, boys, and take this money home to our parents." They nodded, speechless, and began following Wink.

The boys' folks all said the money wasn't rightfully theirs and turned it over to the authorities, who discovered the money was from a bank robbery the old man had pulled off. The bank was grateful to get their $100,000 back and gave each boy a reward, $100 each, which was like a million dollars to their families.

From then on, Wink was a legend. Folks passed the story down through generations of how Wink had turned into some kind of beast like a grizzly bear and ran the bank robber off.

As time went on and the story was handed down through generations, the story became that Wink actually became a grizzly bear, while some say he tore the man's arm off and chased him for miles while he screamed for mercy.

No bullies in school ever messed with Wink again, after that. Even when Wink was an adult, people went out of their way to be sure they didn't rile up ole Wink Sizemore. Folks both feared and respected Wink until the day he died.

NIGHT SHIFT

Garrett Clifton

I worked the night shift at a small business at the time. It wasn't the most popular. Just a little hole in the wall. A small gas station away from most of the town, but we did a lot of business.

It was late one night, and I got stuck working the late hours of the graveyard shift. Not that I really minded. There was extra pay, and I needed the money. There wasn't much going on, so I was screwing around on my phone, texting friends, playing games, and whatnot.

I shoved my phone into my pocket, because it had gotten to about four percent of battery life left. I then happened to look up in the round mirror hanging in one of the corners from the ceiling and noticed someone standing in one of the aisles. I couldn't see what they looked like with their hoodie covering the majority of their body. It appeared that they were wearing a brown hoodie, baggy blue jeans, and sneakers.

It kind of frightened me at first. because I thought that I was the only person in the store, and normally the bell would ding if somebody came in. But I figured that maybe I had been so concentrated on my phone that maybe I just hadn't paid any attention to realize that someone had actually entered the store, so I didn't hear the bell go off. I was embarrassed more than anything, me being in the store with a customer, and I was on my phone. I decided to walk over to the person to see if they needed any assistance.

I shuffled my way over to them and turned the corner, when I saw them. I hollered at them, asking them if they needed help finding anything. There was no response. They appeared to be zoned out, as if they were in their own world or something. The person appeared to be a bit stocky and fairly tall, tall enough that they towered over me. I couldn't tell what they looked like, as they kept their face hidden with their hood and had their hands stuffed into their pockets. I figured that maybe they just wanted to be left alone to do their own shopping, so I blew it off and told them that if they had any questions not to hesitate to ask.

I turned and walked away, but just as soon as I turned the corner of the aisle, I heard a loud crash. I ran back around to see what the commotion was but was taken aback when I saw that some products had been knocked over on the floor. But... no one was there. The person I had seen moments ago had been standing in the center of the aisle. I questioned if it were possible for the person to have fled to another aisle. It would only make sense.

I went and picked up all the products and placed them back on the shelf. I scoured the rest of the store, but with no luck. I figured that whoever did that must have left the store, although I couldn't see how, since I would have for sure heard the bell go off.

I was starting to get a little paranoid now. I wasn't sure if our bell had broken or what was going on. *Where did this person disappear to?* I wondered to myself, as I made my way back behind the register trying to make sense of it.

A few minutes passed by, and I realized that it was around closing, so I packed up my stuff and decided to use the bathroom before I left, since it was about a twenty-five-minute drive back to my house. I grabbed the keys to the employee bathroom and headed towards the hallway leading to the bathrooms. I walked up to the blue metal door and stuck the key in and gave it a solid turn as I heard the lock click, and I shoved the door open. I walked in and locked the door behind me.

While sitting quietly on the round porcelain, I heard a light tap on the door. At first, I thought that I was just hearing things, so I dismissed it, not thinking anything of it. But then, the tapping changed to a loud pounding, followed with the sound of the door handle jiggling. Someone was trying to get in. I wasn't totally alarmed right away, as I had thought that it was probably just a customer that desperately needed to use the restroom, so I proceeded to tell them that there was another bathroom further down the hall that was for customers. But the pounding just continued.

My body began to run cold with fear as I could somehow sense that something was wrong. I could feel it. I quickly finished my business, and then I quietly inched close to the door. Suddenly, the banging stopped. I was scared now. Something was definitely wrong.

I pulled my phone out to call the police, but my phone was dead from messing around on it all day. "Great. Just my luck," I said to myself as I nearly threw my phone at the wall out of anger.

I looked around for something to use as a weapon, since I knew I was trapped, and the only way to get out of here was through the bathroom door. I came up with nothing, but thankfully, I had my car keys on me. I knew that if I could make it out the front of the store, I'd be able to get out of there, and I'd be home free.

I saw a small trash can in the left corner next to the sink and decided to use that as a projectile, if needed. I picked up the small trash can and prepared myself for whatever might happen next. I took a deep breath and reluctantly unlocked the door. With the trashcan in one hand, I used my other to swing open the door and then run out.

I sprinted towards the entrance of the store and nearly tripped over myself as I saw the same silent person wearing the same brown hoodie I had seen before. They were waiting for me with what appeared to be a scornful look on their face. I couldn't quite tell, so I wasn't sure. I still couldn't make out any distinct features about the individual.

They were wearing gloves to cover their hands and masks that partially covered their faces. They had eye makeup around their eyes and covering the parts of their mouths that were visible. I saw the stranger make a quick motion towards me in my direction, and I immediately threw the trash can at them as I ran out of the store. I rushed to my car as I pulled my keys out of my pocket and unlocked it.

I flung the door open, stuck the key in the ignition, shifted gears and drove off. But as soon as I did this, I heard a loud grinding – thumping-like noise. The sound pierced my ears as my car began to dogleg on me. I had to pull over to see what was wrong. I quickly got out to check and see what the problem was.

That was when it hit me like a brick. Someone had slashed my front driver's side tire. The rubber had been completely ripped off, and my tire was thrashed. My stomach sank when I saw a pair of headlights turn on out in the distance. There were no other cars down this remote road except mine and the one that I had just spotted. I knew they were coming for me. The headlights only got bigger and brighter as they drew closer to me.

I got sick when I realized that I was too far from any houses or neighborhoods to seek help. I looked off into the distance and saw a dirt trail that I could follow and hopefully escape them. I shut the driver door and locked my car as I then began to run down the dirt trail, hoping that the vehicle wouldn't follow.

I ran for what felt like hours when I saw some thick bushes over to my left. I dove into the green shrubbery and hid and waited. I waited desperately and looked around for about five minutes until I finally decided that it was safe. Just as I was about to move, I saw a vehicle slowly drive down the dirt trail. It had its headlights off and was moving at an incredibly slow pace. Even though it was dark, I was still able to vaguely define the vehicle as it drew close. I nearly broke down when I saw that it was a white windowless van.

Everything was silent as the van began to pass by, but I could faintly hear the sound of a window being rolled down as I held my hand over my mouth, trying to stay quiet as I stayed still. I waited for a few minutes until the van had turned its headlights back on, and it finally left. I decided to remain hidden for a few more minutes before leaving my position.

I checked to see if the coast was clear, and I didn't see anything. I then ran for miles down a path that was unknown to me until I reached the closest house I could find. I started banging on the door until someone came to help.

An elderly woman answered the door, and I explained what was going on. I asked her if I could come in, but she whispered to me in a soft voice, that wasn't a good idea. I was puzzled by this. The woman then brought me a phone to dial 911. I noticed her hand trembling as I took the phone from her.

After making my call, the lady pointed off to the distance as she proceeded to whisper to me "Go wait over there. Out of the light." That struck me as odd. I wasn't sure why I was told to do this. Though I wasn't sure, the fear in me made it easy to conform. I walked down to the area the woman had pointed to and waited behind some trees.

While I waited, I noticed an old barn over on

my right. The doors were about half-way open, as if someone had tried to close them but didn't quite get it all the way. I leaned forward to get a closer view, and as I did, I could see something inside. I froze in horror as my eyes adjusted to the darkness, and I saw what it was that was in the barn. It was the white windowless van! It couldn't have been the same one from before. It just couldn't!

That's when I went to get a closer look, and my eyes grew wide as my hand touched it. It was warm. I knew that this was the van that had been following me. There was no doubt in my mind. I then darted into a nearby forest and ran for miles, taking twists and curves on an endless lap until I finally reached a more populated area.

I flagged down the first car I saw, and thankfully, they stopped. I explained what was going on, and they gave me a ride to the nearest convenience store where I called the police for a second time. When the police came, I explained what had happened and we went back to my work to search for my car, but when we got there, it was nowhere to be found. This didn't make sense.

I knew I didn't drive it any further after finding out that my tire had been slashed, because I didn't want to mess up the rim any more than it already was. And I didn't even drive all that far, anyway.

So where could it have gone? I wondered to myself as I tried to discern the situation. The police dropped me off at my house and told me that they would further their investigation on my car's whereabouts in the morning and that if they found anything, they would contact me to let me know.

The next morning, I awoke to the police calling to tell me that they had found my car. But what they told me had sent a haunting aura through my body that disturbed me. They had found it about twenty miles away from the gas station!

I knew that I hadn't driven that far. And when I went to go look at it, the rim was completely trashed. Someone had driven my car. But who? And how? The police and I went back to the gas station to see if I could remember the path that I took to get to the elderly woman's house, to retrace my steps. I couldn't remember. It had been dark, and I had taken all kinds of different turns and twists as I ran. And I didn't know where I was going at the time. The place that I had gone was uncharted to me until last night. I couldn't remember. I tried, but I just couldn't.

The police said that they would do some more investigating and see if they couldn't uncover anything else. I thanked them and then called my boss and told her about what had happened, since I was too shaken up to call the night before.

My boss started flipping out after hearing the words that were coming out of my mouth. She offered to give me time off and to raise my pay, but I told her that I couldn't work there anymore after what I'd experienced.

A few weeks passed, and I ended up getting a new job somewhere else. I never heard anything more from the police, so I can only guess that they never caught the man... or woman... who was with me that night at the gas station. And now, anytime I see a white van or hear strange noises within the night, I always wonder to myself *Is that them?*

JENNIFER'S GHOSTS

A. Tuna Dobbins

Jennifer has a weird feeling about today. She can't put her finger on it, but she knows that something is about to happen. As she walks out to her car, she looks both ways before going around to the driver's door. There are no vehicles moving on the street.

What's going on? Why am I feeling weird about today? she thinks.

After getting into her car and starting the engine, she hears tires screeching and almost jumps out of her skin, when a small sedan flies by her driver's door sideways. The small sedan slams into the car behind her and spins back into the middle of the street.

"Oh! My! Gawd!" she says out loud. She looks into the rearview mirror, and the sliding car spins to a stop. She can't tell if there is anyone in the car, because of all the white smoke from the air bags.

Jenni jumps out of her car with her cell phone and runs over to the other car. The white smoke is starting to settle, and she sees a man in the driver's seat. Jenni knocks on the window and yells, "Are you okay?"

The man doesn't respond. Jenni keys in 9-1-1 on her cell phone and hears more tire screeching noises. She jumps toward the curb, as a police car slides to a stop not far from her.

"Emergency response. What's your emergency?"

"I just saw a car wreck on my street, and the guy inside isn't talking to me. A police car just slid to a stop nearby, also."

"Can I have your name and the address of this accident?" the 9-1-1 operator asks.

"Jennifer Wymans. 12301 South Chisholm Way." Jenni answers, as she watches the officer run over to the wrecked car with his gun drawn. The officer breaks the driver's door glass with a hammer of some sort and points his gun at the driver.

"Hands up where I can seem them!" the officer screams. The man in the car does not respond. The officer looks at the man in the car, before lowering his gun a little.

"Did you say 12301 South Chisholm?" the 9-1-1 operator asks.

"Yes! Yes, I did. The officer just broke out the man's window and is pointing a gun at the man. What's going on?"

"Is the car with the man in it a black or dark blue Nissan sedan?"

Jenni looks at the car for a few seconds. It is a dark Nissan sedan. "Yes," she answers.

"We've been chasing that car for several miles now. The man in it carjacked that car and shot the owner less than an hour ago. There are more officers on the way. Please stand by, and do not leave. They will want to ask you some questions."

Jenni stammers a little but agrees to stand by.

After other officers appear, the carjacking suspect is pulled from the car and handcuffed. Jenni can hear him groan, as he is handcuffed. Jenni can see blood on the man's back and shoulders. When the ambulance arrives, the man is still lying on his stomach and moaning.

One officer questions Jenni. After learning that the only thing Jenni saw was the out-of-control car slide by her and hear it hit the car behind her, they let her go.

Jenni calls her boss to let him know that she will be a little late getting to work.

Whew, that was close, she thinks as she drives away.

When Jenni gets to the parking lot at her office, the weird feeling of something bad happening hits her again. She looks all around the parking lot before walking inside.

Before she can relax, there is a crashing noise

around the corner of the foyer; then there is a lot of dust and smoke. She and others rush toward the smoke and see the elevator doors cocked at odd angles, with a little gape between then.

As the dust clears, Jenni can see a couple of people lying on the floor of the elevator, and the elevator floor is about three feet below the ground floor. A lady in the elevator starts to move and then screams. Her leg is twisted at an odd angle.

Jenni looks away. She hears someone nearby talking to the 9-1-1 operator. Not long after that, officers and EMTs arrive. The elevator doors are pried open, and the man and woman inside are helped out.

Jenni is again questioned about what she saw and heard. Once the officers realize that Jenni didn't see anything, they let her leave.

While there are other elevators in the building, Jenni walks over to the stairs at the end of the foyer. She climbs the six floors to her office.

"You won't believe what's happened to me today," she says to a coworker.

After telling her story a couple of times, she sits down at her desk. "Well that's over now. Nothing else is going to happen to me or near me today," she says.

But Jenni is wrong.

Just before her lunch break, everyone hears the news about the people injured in the elevator. The lady's leg was badly broken, and the man in the elevator received bruises and maybe whiplash from the fall.

Just before leaving for lunch, Jenni checks the local news outlets on her cell phone. The highspeed chase report says that the man in the Nissan had exchanged gunfire with police before he wrecked the car on a neighborhood street. The report says that he died from the gunshot wounds he received during the chase.

Jenni puts her face in her hands and closes her eyes for several seconds.

"What's for lunch?" a co-worker asks.

"I don't know. Let's go down to the street and see how busy the restaurants are." Jenni answers.

There are several restaurants at street level in the area. Jenni and her co-worker walk to the corner where there is a Mexican place and an Asian place. Jenni points to the Asian place, and her coworker nods in agreement.

During lunch, the hair on the back of Jenni's neck seems to stand up and tingle. "Oh, no. Something bad is about to happen," she says.

"Something bad? What do you mean?" her co-worker asks.

"I'm getting that tingling feeling, just like I did this morning when the car chase ended on my street and when the elevator fell. If I had been standing in the street beside my car, that car would have hit me. Then when I got to the building, I got that tingling feeling again. I looked around the parking lot before coming inside. If I had gotten into the building sooner, I would have been on that elevator. Now, I'm getting that tingling feeling again."

"What's about to happen?"

"I don't know. I just feel that something bad is about to happen. I don't know what it is, but I wish I knew."

About then, a car crashes into the Mexican place. Jenni and her friend look out the windows of the restaurant and see people scrambling from the Mexican restaurant. Jenni can only shake her head.

"I told you something bad was about to happen. I'm glad you like Asian food," Jenni says.

"I'm staying next to you today. That's the third time something bad has happened near you but not to you," the co-worker says.

"Spooky."

"Yeah." The co-worker nods as sirens are heard approaching.

Later, back at the office, Jenni checks the local news outlets on her cell phone. Three people were injured when the car crashed into the Mexican place. The report goes on to say that the driver thought his ex-girlfriend was in there, and he was trying to kill her. It turns out that the ex-girlfriend was in the Asian place, not far from them. Jenni shows this to her co-worker.

"Wow!"

"Yeah, wow!"

The rest of the afternoon, Jenni is looking over her shoulder every time someone or something makes a noise. She hasn't had any more tingling feelings, but she's got the jumps now.

Walking out into the parking lot to go home, Jenni is on high alert. Nothing happens. The drive home is totally uneventful…until she turns onto her street.

That tingling feeling starts again. The accident from this morning has long since been cleaned up, and her neighbor's car has been hauled away. Jenni carefully parks her car on the street in front of her house. She looks both ways several times before getting out.

Jenni walks over to her mailbox and pulls the lid down. There are several pieces of mail inside. When she sticks her hand inside to grab the mail, she gets a very sharp pain in her middle finger. She jerks her hand out of the mailbox and sees blood all over her hand. Her face goes pale.

Oh No! She thinks as she faints.

She hits her head on the edge of the mailbox on the way down and puts a huge gash in her scalp. Her mailbox is made of brick and stands about four feet tall. The mailbox doesn't move when she hits it, and she hasn't moved since hitting the ground.

A neighbor that lives just down the street sees Jenni lying on the ground next to her mailbox. He stops in the middle of the street and dashes over to Jenni. There is blood all around her head from the gash in her scalp. He dials 9-1-1.

He can see that Jenni is breathing and still alive, but she is bleeding badly from the head wound. He yells at the 9-1-1 dispatcher to get an ambulance there as fast as she can.

About the time the EMTs are loading her into their ambulance, Jenni starts to regain consciousness.

"Where am I?" she mumbles.

"Miss Wymans, you've been in an accident, and we're going to take you to the hospital," an EMT answers.

"My head hurts like hell. What happened?" she asks rather groggily.

"You hit your head on the edge of that brick mailbox in front of your house. You've lost some blood and you may have a concussion. We have you hooked up to an IV to replenish the fluids that you lost." The EMTs roll the gurney into the ambulance.

The second EMT asks, "Do you remember what you were doing before you slipped and fell?"

Jenni stares at the EMT for several seconds, blinks her eyes several times like she is trying to clear her head. "I was trying get my mail, and something bit my hand." Jenni raises her right hand, and there is a bandage on the middle finger. "Do you know what bit me?"

The EMTs exchange looks; then one says, "We found some blood on the edge of an envelope in the mailbox. It looks like you got a bad paper cut when you reached for your mail."

"A paper cut!" she yells back at them.

"That's what it looks like. By the way, we left the mail in the box. You can pick it up after you see the doctors in ER and leave the hospital. The gouge on your head is going to require a few stitches."

Jenni closes her eyes. "After all I've lived through today, I get a papercut and hit my head."

She closes her eyes and tries to replay the day in her head. The car crash right in front of her house rolls by. The dust and smoke from the elevator falling. The car crashing into the restaurant across the street from her. Then the mailbox scene and the paper cut.

Seeing the blood on her hand makes her feel like her time has finally come. She remembers feeling faint, then nothing else until she woke up on the gurney.

Jenni spends the night in the hospital under observation. The next morning, the doctors report that they are not seeing any evidence of a concussion, and they release her. She has eight stitches in her head and a small bandage on her finger, plus one hell of a headache.

After taking a cab back to her house, Jenni carefully reaches into the mailbox and removes the mail. She flips through it and finds one envelope with blood on it. The flap has not been sealed, and that is where she got the paper cut.

Jenni opens the envelope and sees that is a solicitation from a psychic reader wanting to tell her fortune for the small sum of fifty dollars.

"The last thing I need or want is to have some psychic reader tell my fortune. I'm already having premonitions about what things are about to happen around me. I don't need some charlatan telling me what I already know."

Jenni looks around the street and then at her house. The tingling feeling is gone. *At least for now.*

THE OLD RUIN

Rosemarie Sabel Durgin

The building was next to the only movie theater in town. We children passed by the house daily on our way to and from school. There the ruin stood, for years after the war. The house had once been a restaurant, a *"Gasthaus."* The stately structure had been on that corner for more than a hundred years.

There was still the smell of beer lingering about the building. One could smell the yeast on days when the humidity was just right. The owners had once brewed the golden liquid and sold it to their guests. Old timers in town remembered drinking the liquid, and they claimed that Zangerle's beer was much better than the now famous brew of the big brewery in town, the Simon *Bräu.* And that beer had been brewed much longer than the newcomer at the other end of downtown.

Yes, that building had occupied that corner of the main street in town for a long time, more than a hundred years. The corner had even been named after the little Brewery; Zangerle's *Eck*, until Christmas day 1944. The house, like most of the buildings in town, had been destroyed by a massive bombing raid of the Allies, as they attempted to destroy the last defenses of the German Reich. The town of Bitburg and thus, Zangerle's brewery and *Gasthaus,* had ceased to exist that day.

We children passed by the ruin daily, and often, we would be thinking of what might have happened to the people who once lived there. No one knew what had become of them.

Some of the more adventurous boys would try and explore the crumbling structure, looking for a bottle of that beer that had survived the bombing. Maybe they could find some sort of memento. After so many years after the war, that was a slim possibility. Still they searched, and their friends would stay and watch and look out for the town's police officer, to warn them of his approach. Going into the ruins was strictly *verboten*, because the likelihood of further collapse was great. The boys never found much. Nevertheless, they searched and hoped for a bottle of beer, no small task, either.

Walking past that building was eerie, though. In the fall and winter, as strong winds played around the ruin, one could almost hear people calling for help. We girls shuddered at that and tried to avoid going past the ruin. We would take the way across the bus station, which was also fraught with danger, because one had to dart between the moving buses. The boys, however, were laughing at us, calling us scaredy cats. We did not mind that. The thought of people still being alive down there in the subbasement was scary indeed. Or were the ghosts of the inhabitants that perished that day still calling to be released from their imprisonment in the ruin? We could only imagine.

Then, on a fine day in the summer of 1953, just a few days before summer vacation, a construction crew arrived at the old ruin. They were dismantling what was left of a once proud building.

The next day in school, the story was on everyone's lips. It was a grizzly story, indeed. The bodies of five people had been found down in what was once the bomb shelter of that building. The identification of the skeletons took a long time. The boys were chagrined. The thought that they had perhaps stepped on someone's body was more than a little disconcerting. We girls now knew that the ghosts could rest, and we would never hear their moans again.

THE ANCIENT MOUNTAIN STATUES

Debbie Fogle

The trail is a long hike up to an unknown artifact destination. I am an adventurous traveler, but times are getting crazy for a solo traveler. I try to find unusual places to see in order to have an experience no one else can have. Now, I am in the high terrain of an ancient mountain, anxiously waiting to see a gem of a mountain.

The *Puscopoteet* stone carving collection isn't in any of the tourist brochures. This is why the museum doesn't have a high visitor count. If you are paying attention on the first trail, you will stumble onto the stone carving on the second trail.

Puscopoteet became famous for the thirty-foot god-like statues found in the mountains. The discovery of the statues came after several blasts of dynamite revealed a head of the first of seven statues on three mountains. The smaller stone statues are twenty minutes from the larger ones. The guide also states the thirty-foot carvings are statues that can't be uncovered one hundred percent, because the mountains would collapse, causing mass destruction for the entire community below the mountains.

I purchase a pass to go see the massive

carvings but stumble upon an archway that catches my eye. I take several photos of the warning signs along the entrance, at first, thinking the humor of the warnings are a simple joke. I view sign, after sign, after sign, warning all visitors, NOT to touch the statues. Six computer screens used for signing in the museum flash warning messages every three seconds.

"I get it!" I mumble to myself. "Don't touch the statues!"

I'm directed to a counter to scan my passport into the system and have my photo taken. I smile for the camera and receive a ticket. *If only airport travel was that easy,* I think.

DO NOT TOUCH STATUES in red ink is printed on my ticket. I am directed to a door, and I slip my ticket into the ticket slot, again am warned not to touch the statues. I proceed down the walkway to an outdoor opening, revealing the seven statues and their meanings.

The iridescent statue is moonstone and represents good fortune. The orange vibrant statue is citrine and represents success. The pink statue is rose quartz and represents love. The blue statue is blue kainite and represents calming to the whole being. The purple statue is mica and diminishes anger. The green statue is jade and inspires ambition. The black statue is black obsidian and bring the spiritual protector.

The brochure explains the riches for the people are provided by the riches from the mountain. I am in awe of the beauty of the statues and sit down in a corner to view them all, and as I sit there, I feel a sense of serenity and worthiness, a reason for living. It's like the blood in my veins grows stronger, and I finally have a purpose for living, but then . . .

The three youngsters stumble out of the tunnel talking loudly, pushing each other around, like ten-year-olds. I emphasize "youngsters" as a joke, I myself am only twenty-five years of age but feel old as I watch them

"Get back, dude!" one shouts.

"Hey, dude. I love you," another responds with a fit of laughter.

Oh hell, there goes my serene visit, I think.

I do hate loud people on tours. A temple of sacred artifacts shouldn't be violated with loud voices and rude behavior. If I were a four-hundred-year-old statue, I would be upset at the rude people and their unacceptable behavior.

"What the f***, dudes?" the yellow tennis shoe guy blurts out.

"These are some sexy as f*** statues," the green tennis shoe guy declares.

"Damn! These babes got it all in the right places," the black tennis shoe guy laughs, then spits out a wade of gum onto the grassy area in front of the green statue.

The three rude obnoxious boys haven't noticed me sitting on a bench in the corner of the courtyard.

"Take my picture with the blue one." The yellow tennis shoe guy hands his phone to the green tennis shoe guy.

"DUDE! Don't go beyond the barriers. Follow the rules," the green tennis shoe guys orders.

"F*** the rules! Who's gonna see us? Do you see any video cameras out here?" The yellow tennis shoe guy twirls around and spots me sitting in the corner.

"You the useless security?" He laughs at his own question.

"Nope. Just a tourist trying to enjoy the statues," I remark.

"Well, keep your mouth shut, because we are taking pictures with these bitchin' statues."

Yellow tennis shoe guy snorts, "Get it!" Snorting again, "A bitchin' statue, because all the statues are women. I bet you're disappointed, huh? Or are you some kind of lesbian?"

I wave my hand in the air. "Do your thing and leave me alone." I pick up the brochure and begin reading about the red statue, noticing the thirty-five

DO NOT TOUCH THE STATUE warnings emphasized throughout the entire brochure. As I place the brochure into my backpack, I glance up to witness the young men assaulting the statues in a grotesque manner.

The green tennis shoe guy is humping on the front of the green statue. The black tennis shoe guy is pretending to lick the nipple of the blue statue, and the yellow tennis shoe guy is snaking his body around the legs of the black statue.

"Rock solid," yellow tennis shoe guy chimes in as his hands ravage the polished onyx.

I snap. "Stop that, you idiot! Have some respect!" I yell at them.

"Shut up!" they yell in unison at me.

I grab my backpack and decide to visit the statues another time and desperately look for an exit sign.

Finally spotting the sign for the exit, I make my way through a rock archway. The rock archway brings me into a cavern full of jewels, jewels the size of my hands, and the same colors of the statues. I still don't see an exit door, but I'm amazed at the brilliant colors of the stones surrounding me.

I become slightly panicked, thinking I will be stuck inside the exhibit with the three obnoxious boys, but the moment I think my fate will be with the boys, is the moment the boys rudely stumble to where I am standing.

"Oh, it's you again. Thought you left," green tennis shoe guy laughs.

"I'm trying," I snarl, not meaning to be rude to them, but their behavior is disgusting.

"Damn, my skin itches," the yellow tennis shoe guy complains.

"Wimp. Did you put on your sunny-wunny sunscreen?" In a baby voice, the green tennis shoe guy smarts off.

"No. This is different, dude." Raising his arm, the yellow tennis shoe guy displays a strange rash on his arms. "Look at this crap!" He cries out in a complete state of panic.

Right before my eyes, yellow tennis shoe guy's arms turn into a shiny black stone. The weight of his arms drop him to the floor in a second.

"What the f***?" green tennis shoe guy yells out.

I turn around to a new horrific scene: Green tennis shoe guy's skin on his legs are changing to a sea green stone.

"My legs! What in the hell?" he yells, as we all, wide-eyed, look at his torso of human flesh, but his legs are solid jade.

I frantically look down at my legs and quickly

run my fingers over my arms. I'm not even sunburned from all the walking in the sun. No discolorations on my body.

"Man, I don't feel well. Let's get out of here and find a clinic," he suggests, but his body isn't moving.

"Good idea. Let's find a clinic." Black tennis shoe guy's face is frozen. "I cannnnn't mooove." He murmurs the words as the blue color envelopes the skin on his neck. He too suddenly drops to the floor, unable to move.

Yellow tennis shoe guy murmurs, "What is going onnnnnn?" Spittle drops from his lips, and tears flow from his eyes and drop onto the shining onyx.

I kneel down in front of the young men, and the shine from the jewels around the room catch my eyes again. The piles and piles of jewels are just lying around the temple, "No it can't be." I whisper to myself. "It's not possible."

"Heeee meeeee!" The green tennis shoe guy's muffled cries are misunderstood.

All three young boys are solid jeweled statues, splayed out on the ground before me.

"Hello." I call out.

Just then, a computer screen near a door lights up, "Thank you for visiting the *Puscopoteet* Museum. Please exit now."

"Hello. There is something really wrong here." I call out to the empty museum hall.

"Please exit now," the recorded voice repeats.

"But, I..." Just then, all three statues on the ground crumble into piles of magnificent jewels, right before my eyes. I run to the exit door, and a woman in a colorful dress and headdress hands me a cloth bag.

"Thank you for following the rules of our ancient temple. Have a nice day." She escorts me toward the exit gateway and to the tut-tut car boarding area.

"Boarding now," a man calls out from a small tut-tut car.

I climb into the small tut-tut, and the man begins pedaling fast, and as we roll down the dirt road, I see a man pushing a wheel barrel full of shimmering stones. I slowly untie the string on my cloth bag and peek inside to see several large shining jewels.

"Thank you for obeying the rules, Miss," the man whispers.

I grip my bag of jewels tightly with a terror deep in my soul.

IN THE LIFE LIBRARY

Andrea Foster

I put another one in the room, put the helmet called the Brain Scoop on his head, and turned on the machine.

Most folks come to have the process done just before they are going to die, to save their life story for the grandkids and posterity. Some come when they find out they have Alzheimer's, because they want their memories saved before they lose them.

But on occasion, a young one comes, who wants to forget everything, and then he or she donates his life story to the Life Library, and then starts life afresh, without past negative hurts and pains and traumas that can keep a person from wanting to go on.

This one was young, and the sadness and despondency in his body language—and the look on his face--illustrated that he wanted to forget something, come out new, with no memories of what had been before.

I asked him if he was sure, and he said yes evenly, almost sternly. He must have been homeless, because he was carrying a bag—heavy, almost like a laundry bag, with him — a heavy burden, as though all his life were in there.

"Let's do it!" he called, severe in his tone, stronger than I thought he'd be. I turned on the machine. It hummed and shook and only took five minutes to rid the brain of its memories and transfer them to a document, which I could then put on file, to be printed later as an on-demand book from our Life Library. The machine shuddered and shook at the end and then stopped.

I guessed,, *it's done!* I unhooked the young man and looked at him. He was happy, mindless, smiling.

"Thank you!" he said almost wonderingly, getting up and stumbling out of the room, moving away slowly and beginning to whistle a tune rather joyfully.

"Wait!" I called. "You forgot your bag!"

He was gone already. I went to the bag, noticing it beginning to turn black with a dark wetness. *Uh-oh, Blood!*

I opened the bag. All I saw was his head — an old man, bleeding from the mouth. I undid the bag to see if he could be saved or was alive. No pulse. He had a steak knife stuck through his heart, straight through a T- shirt that proclaimed, "World's Worst Boss."

I wondered if his story would be on the Life Book.

Only trouble is…the perpetrator was no more…memory wiped clean, new life to create with a new name. I dialed 911 anyway.

ANTICIPATION

Les McDermott

Mary Jane creeped up to the window and carefully pulled the curtain open just enough to peek out. The street was dark in front of their house, but down at the corner, several people were chanting and jumping around under the streetlight. Smoke drifted down the street from the car that was on fire.

Sirens were blasting in the distance. Then, flashing lights busted onto the scene in front of her house. The sirens vibrated the window and scared the daylights out of Mary Jane. Six-year-old Mary Jane was trying to make sense out of the chaos of the unrest. She had seen it on TV, but now in real life, it was outside her window. After getting out from under the coffee table, still shaken from the siren, she looked around for her parents. Her mom was behind the couch, and Dad was in the closet, trying to find his hunting rifle. He had thrown boxes and clothes out on the floor and still hadn't gotten the rifle. Her brother came running into the living room, wondering what was going on.

"Are we getting invaded by aliens?" Douglas

yelled. Douglas was only two years older than Mary, but still didn't understand the riots going on.

Dad hadn't found his rifle, so he ran into the bedroom. Throwing boxes and clothes out of his closet, his rifle fell over and hit him on the head. Grimacing with pain, he picked up the gun. When he got to the front door, he paused to lock and load the rifle. Well, he pulled back the bolt, and there weren't any bullets. Running back into his bedroom, throwing more stuff out of the closet, he found the box of bullets.

By this time, the police car had moved on down the street, and the crowd started to disperse. Out of nowhere, a large group of agitators attacked the police car. The police car started backing up quickly with lights on and siren blasting, and one of the officers was trying to get back into the car.

Dad, now watching out the window, suddenly hollered at his family to get behind him. Yelling and glass breaking noises were coming from outside. Mary Jane and Douglas were huddled behind their mom, and she was huddled behind her husband.

Pointing the rifle at the door in case he had to protect his family, he was ready to pull the trigger. The front window shattered as a bottle flew through, scattering glass all over the floor and the family.

The awful sound of a rifle went off, and

someone screamed outside the house. The crowd got quiet and was stunned, that someone did something to them. After only a few seconds of surprise, the crowd started their rhetoric and started throwing anything and everything at the house.

Dad turned and looked at his family and said calmly, "Go to the back door, but don't go out."

The mother and her kids just huddled down by the back door, when a drastic sound came from the front room. The door had been busted down, and the yelling got louder.

There was another gunshot blast went off, and another, and another. With all the screaming and yelling, it was hard to understand what was being said.

The police siren got closer, and the flashing lights flooded the room. The kids heard the police yell, "Put your weapon down."

Their dad's voice was heard over the noise. "These guys were attacking me and my family!"

A police officer walked into the kitchen where the back door was and saw the family huddled down by the door.

One officer was on the radio calling an ambulance. Another was picking up the rifle. The officer that had walked into the kitchen and saw the family, walked up to the dad and said the most unexpected thing. "You're under arrest for murder."

Surprised, Mom and Dad were just stunned.

The kids didn't understand why Dad was in trouble. They were taking their dad away, after he had saved them from crowd. Seeing their dad put in the police car and driven away, was too much for the kids to comprehend. Even the mother didn't understand. Now, she was left with glass and blood all over the living room and a broken door that was barely hanging on the hinges.

Douglas stood up and asked Mom, "Why did they take Dad?"

HAINT: A TRUE STORY

Melonie B. Hylan

Dear Readers,

To understand this story about ghosts, which Daddy referred to as "haints," (Think "aunts," pronounced "aints."), you have to know something about the story tellers and the people who believed, and still believe, the story.

Bear with me. Out of respect for Daddy and his kin folks, living and dead, I choose not to name names.

Daddy was an imposing, respected authority figure to his family and to others. He indulged himself by reading *The Wall Street Journal*, *Fortune Magazine*, and the Bible. He also limited himself to one highball before dinner and one afterwards. Before I was six, when he had his first heart attack, he liked to hunt and fish, but those days were over. He did not indulge in flights of fancy.

Daddy and his brothers had the advantage of being white men who lived in Louisiana, Texas, and Oklahoma, at a time when they could learn the oil business from the ground up and advance. Daddy was the only member of his family not to graduate from high school, which his family never let him forget. He decked one of his teachers, for what he maintained was a just reason, and never went back. Although he learned not to be as rash as he had been as a teenager, Daddy always remained fearless in the face of disease and any other obstacle in his life. His rise from being a high school dropout, loading oil field pipe onto a truck, to corporate executive might not sound credible, but it was true. My point is, many things that are true sound incredible.

For example, once, in high school, I wrote a description of Daddy's old home place. My grandfather and his friends spent most of their day playing dominoes on a worn card table in the living room, as they dipped snuff and spat into the hearth of the fireplace.

The house, which had not been painted since 1900, sat up on pillars of bricks. As a child, I amused myself by watching the chickens scratching around under the house through the shrunken floorboards. There was no running water, and a bare lightbulb hung from the center of each room. We all drank out of a dipper on the back porch, which hung on a nail beside a galvanized bucket of cool well water. I thought that it was the best water I had ever tasted, but I was terrified of the wasps that built their nests and swarmed around the outhouse.

When my teacher read my essay, she accused

me of writing about something that I had seen on television. She wanted us to write authentic descriptions. Even after I convinced her that I was writing about a real place, she explained that a lot of things may be real, but they are not always believable to readers. I may not have improved my skills on making the truth as believable as fiction, but I am hoping some folks out there, who made it this far, will give me the benefit of the doubt.

As I indicated in the description of the old home place, Daddy grew up as a country boy. By the time that I was going through school in the 1950s and 1960s, Daddy had lost some of his drawl, and he didn't betray as many signs of his country background as he might have at an earlier time. Sometimes his subjects and verbs did not agree, and he still said "foteen" (pronounced with a long "o"), not "fourteen," which my mother found charming.

Daddy had become a successful businessman at age forty. He had always been an entrenched member of the hat-wearing generation. I remember his wearing beautiful, understated suits and smart gray fedora hats every day when he went to work. In the oil fields in the 1920s and 1930s, he had not only worn a hat, but he had even worn a tie with his khakis in the field. He said the hat protected him from the sun, and the closure of the tie at his neck helped keep his body clean. He had chopped cotton, and he knew about being hot and dirty.

As Daddy continued to climb the corporate ladder in the oil business, he occasionally lunched with high ranking politicians. Such men, always men, sat on the board of directors of the multi-national corporation where Daddy held one of the vice-presidencies. Daddy was tall and handsome, and, I am told, he liked a dirty joke. (As his only daughter, I never heard him tell one.) My mother said that Daddy's company used to seat him near John Connolly when the execs went to Dallas, because Connolly appreciated Daddy's humor. (My daddy didn't name drop, and he didn't tell that story. Fortunately, for his sake, Daddy died before Connolly became a Republican.) When Kennedy was assassinated, I remember Daddy being upset. He said that he didn't want to have a president who had bad table manners.

Daddy did, however, believe that some things could not be explained. When he and his family would get together, they loved to tell stories, most of them about local history, or what my mother called gossip. Sometimes, however, they would be about unexplained occurrences, which is the case in the following story. Daddy was also superstitious. He never laid his hat on the bed, for instance, and he taught me when to say "bread and butter," if we were walking alongside each other and something passed between us. As I recall, his were the common folk beliefs, like not walking under a ladder, which I always regarded as good sense, if not good luck.

Daddy and all of his brothers, except for the one who died in World War II, worked for the same company. They were ambitious and hard-working, so we didn't get together as often as the relatives on my mother's side. I also suspected that my daddy's sisters-in-law wanted to keep their distance from my mother. The story of my mother doesn't belong here, but I understand why my aunts might not have liked having her as a guest.

Daddy also had two sisters. (This is important.) The oldest one, who lived to be ninety-nine, was a fabulous cook, which she had learned from my grandmother, who had died before I was born. My grandmother on Daddy's side had heart trouble, no doubt exacerbated by amounts and the quality of her Southern cooking. The youngest sister, who didn't care about cooking or overeating, had a brilliant mind, and she had gone to the University of Arkansas to study math on a scholarship during The Great Depression.

The brothers had helped their little sister, the brainy one, when they could, so that she could become a teacher. Oil field jobs during the Depression were good, solid jobs. Since there was no social safety net or Pell Grants in those days, families had to help each other out. My aunt excelled in college, and she became a high school math teacher. Later, she went back to school and got a master's degree in math and another one in counseling. She was one of the most sensible, down-to-earth persons I ever knew. She believed in evidence and practicality, never in things like haints.

One summer, when I was still in junior high school, my family went on a relatively rare visit to see Daddy's younger brother who lived in Texas. The oil company for which the brothers worked transferred my uncle to a different town, and we were going to see his new home. Working for the company was rather like being in the military. Everyone gave the corporation their utmost loyalty, and the company told its employees where they would live and when they had to move. Sometimes a supervisor got to drive a company car, painted in the company colors. My uncle had bought his new home at a remarkable price, and his family had lived there for nine months.

My uncle's mid-century house was fairly new at that time. His neighborhood was well-kept with neatly mowed lawns and meatball-shaped hedges.

There was just enough space between houses to keep adjacent homeowners from looking into each other's windows. There were brilliant orange and yellow flowers growing along the front of the house, the kind of plants that my family would have had to put inside, if Mother had allowed such things. We lived in Oklahoma, another growing zone.

The architecture of my uncle's new home was modern with a sloping roof that extended over a carport on one side. Everyone entered the house through the kitchen that opened onto the carport instead of going up to the front door. The carport was shady, and the side door was more convenient. People did not go to the front door unless they were someone selling brushes or vacuum cleaners.

Although I never went into the house through that door, I peeked inside the living room once from a hallway. There was a piano and a conventional seating area, which could be completely shut off by doors from the rest of the house. Keeping the room shut off was the custom.

A few other members of Daddy's family, who were out of school for the summer, like my aunt, the math teacher, and another cousin, a Spanish teacher, drove in from out of town to my uncle's place to have a small family reunion. Daddy's oldest brother had already died from chronic illness. Daddy and his younger brother had had their first heart attacks, but they were still popping those nitroglycerin pills and staying the course. The president of the United States had not yet been shot.

I got to spend the night with my cousin, two years my senior, whom I idolized. She was as outgoing as I was shy, and she had beautiful boots with tassels on them that she wore when she performed in her school's drill team. Each boot was a slightly different size, because she had suffered through polio shortly before there was a vaccine. She did all the routines with the other girls, but her mother told me that she didn't do the marching part. I wasn't exactly sure what a drill team was, but I didn't want to ask. I thought that she was fearless and spectacular.

Her older brother was home from college. He went out that afternoon to get a Coke with the Spanish teacher cousin, who also happened to be a talented musician. That night, all of us ate charcoal grilled burgers and hung out in the kitchen. Oddly, we were not invited into the living room to sit around the piano, as we usually did when my musical cousin, the Spanish teacher, was around. My parents were going to stay at a motel, since Daddy needed his sleep. Daddy didn't say that he also wanted to keep the rest of them from hearing him moaning in the night with angina. Perhaps they knew, but I am sure no one minded if my mother, who liked to take on the role of queen bee, also stayed at the motel.

Before my parents left for the night, and once the dishes were done, we gathered in the kitchen. It was not the roomiest place in the house, but it was air-conditioned. The cousins sat on bar stools or on the floor, and the older adults sat around the table, having a highball. My aunt, the math teacher and guidance counselor, didn't drink. She didn't disapprove, but she said that she didn't like the taste. The air was full of cigarette smoke, and there were Fritos, bean dip, and peach cobbler. The room was crowded, but I wanted to sit like my popular girl cousin with my ankles crossed and the skirt of my sundress pulled over my knees, no matter how uncomfortable that position was.

The summer days were long, and the sun was still up when my aunt and uncle began to tell eerie stories about living in their comfortable, modern home. My uncle started out by telling us that he got a great bargain on his new house, because the other people in the neighborhood thought that the house was haunted. Everyone in the kitchen laughed derisively at the ignorance and gullibility of the neighbors.

"But, listen, ya'll have to know that unusual things happen here," my uncle told us. My uncle looked a lot like Daddy, but he spoke louder, acted friendlier, and was definitely more huggable. The plausibility that such a gregarious, happy person would be haunted seemed ludicrous. If he met a haint, I pictured him giving it a friendly slap on the back. "Things move to odd places," he said. "I thought my sweet little wife was playing tricks on me. She likes to have fun." He winked at her.

My aunt playfully stuck out her tongue at him.

"When we first moved in, I would come home from work and not be able to find my reports. Then my better half might find them in the bottom of the laundry basket. We almost had a fight over it one time, but we both swore that we were not trying to fool each other and that neither of us had moved a thing," my uncle continued.

"Sometimes, I move your stuff off the kitchen table when I have to get the kids lunch, and you're not here, but I always put your papers somewhere so that you can find them, like that credenza over there." My aunt pointed to a Blonde Danish modern cabinet under the window. "Then, the children kept complaining that their things were missing. Their socks would be in the trash can, and record albums would turn up behind the rain boots in the closet.

Sister's charm bracelet showed up in the shade of the overhead light fixture. We finally quit accusing each other, and we just learned to live with it."

"Tell them about the shopping trip, hon," my uncle encouraged her.

"Well, the kids were in school, and I went to the grocery store. I wasn't gone long, and when I came back, I unlocked the door to the kitchen and started bringing in the bags and setting them on the table. Then, I thought that I heard a funny noise, coming out of the refrigerator. So, I opened up the door, and our two chihuahua dogs were in the vegetable bins. I got them out, and they were all right, but I was so upset that we had to eat peanut butter sandwiches that night."

"That was chilling, no pun intended," my musical cousin said, and everyone laughed, but we admitted that it was a disturbing story.

Early the next morning, Mother and Daddy came back from the motel, and we all met in the kitchen for breakfast. My uncle had on a ruffled apron and was cooking up bacon and eggs with hash browns and pancakes. Daddy teased him about the apron, but my uncle was unfazed. He loved feeding everyone. He said that he loved to bring his wife coffee on his day off and let her stay in her dressing gown. My aunt, the math teacher, was helping him serve up plates, and we all perched at different places around the kitchen to eat breakfast.

When we sat down, my math-teacher aunt, who had spent the night in the living room on the couch, said that she had something that she wanted to tell everyone. "I love all of you, and I will come back to visit, but I will never stay in that room again. There was someone in there with me all night, keeping me awake, and I wasn't able to get any sleep."

Everyone was stunned. My aunt never lied. She didn't play practical jokes. Whatever had kept her awake could never be explained.

Within a decade, both Daddy and my uncle would die from their heart disease. Open heart surgery had come to the United States, but the two brothers' cases were too far advanced for surgery to do them much good. My uncle died on the operating table. Daddy, who never quite recovered from his bypass, died shortly afterwards in a flu epidemic. After Daddy's two sisters died, the families drifted apart.

What haunted me for years was losing touch with my cousins on Daddy's side of the family, although I have to say losing touch was not entirely their fault. Now, only one of them is left. My beautiful, smart "girl" cousin is an administrator in a large health plex in Houston, and we found each other on Facebook. Some of my cousins' children actually located me, and I have visited them and met some of their children. Someday, I want to drive down to south Texas again and see if I can find that unassuming house. I wonder if anyone else ever lived in it.

As far as I know, Daddy's family only has this one haint story left, but those of us who were there all believed it, and I'm passing it on.

GRANDMOTHER'S WARDROBE

Lynn Dell Jones

That smell of perfume haunted me. It fluttered through the air, teasing my senses, leading me towards an unforeseen end. I ran down hallways covered in red tapestries, my night gown shuddering as I ran in the cold. Moonlight streaming in the stained windows, showed me the way as I searched for the perfume's source. I ran around blind corners, through handmade doorways of solid tooled oak, into rooms once filled with laughter and terrible deeds.

With each step, the scent grew stronger. Roses, a sting of ginger and citrus. I couldn't quite put my finger on the familiarity of it, it was always a memory just out of reach.

As I went from room to room, I entered a grand chamber, a room of terrible deeds. This old room differed from the rest. It had one solitary candle that sat in a pewter candle holder by a large four poster bed. The light cascaded out, revealing a room dark, heavy and menacing. The floor was cold, the wood warped slightly and splintered. My bare feet lost what little heat they once held.

A huge fireplace lay opposite the bed, unlit,

dark from years of soot, devoid of life, and above it, a large portrait dominated the room. In the painting, a woman sat, wearing a magnificent dark turquoise dress of many decades long ago. Her dark hair was pulled tightly in a bun, her pale skin like languid pearl, and her eyes cold, cruel with dispassion and deception.

Those eyes seemed to watch and follow me as I wandered around the bed until I stood at its foot. A once rich, now faded crimson blanket covered the down mattress, and as the candlelight struggled against an unseen draft, it became clear that someone lay in the bed.

I could not see the face of this person, the body was covered from head to foot by the red blanket, shrouded by it. The sight of that cloth outline struck fear into my mind and heart, I dared not touch or remove the blanket, uncertain that my nerves could endure the shock of what laid beneath. Again, I was stung by the familiarity of it all, a memory hiding in the shadows just out of sight, refusing to reveal itself.

The pungent rose perfume was stronger than it had been before, as I could feel the spiteful gaze of the portrait behind me, watching me. Then I noticed another scent. Something which had festered in that room for years, obscured by the sweetness of the perfume, a lewd underbelly, a foul stench.

As I stared at the outline of head and body beneath the blanket, the stench grew. With each breath, I was treated to a mixture of roses and something humid; murky, like mildew after a downpouring of rain. There was something rotten in that room with me. The rancid smell became so thick that I could taste it. The hidden memory threatened to break loose from its gilded cage. I had to flee, I had to run, be as far away from that room, that house, out into the open where I could breathe again.

I walked quickly to the door where I had entered. It was locked. I twisted at the metal handle; its spherical body shone from decades of use. The locked oak door echoed out into distant recesses of vacated halls which taunted me and resisted. I was a prisoner confined to this single room, to a place where the sweet air of flowers was mixed with that of death and disgust.

I pounded on the door, shouted, screamed. But my pleas went unanswered. They simply faded into lonely recesses. A house, my family home which I had not visited since I was seven. A family home that was overgrown with Spanish moss that hung from the cypress and tupelo trees of the deep bayou swamps of Louisiana. A place which hid dark recollections, and wounds which ran deep, covered thinly by the preceding decades. At last, I gave in. I stopped my protests, rested my forehead on the cold wooden surface of the locked door, and tried to compose myself.

Then I heard a sound.

One at first, followed by three others. It was a clicking, creaking noise. I turned around slowly to see what was there, but the room was as it had been. The body in the bed lay still, the blanket forming a perfect impression of it.

The bedside candle flickered but remained lit, and as it did, shadows danced around the room. They created the illusion of movement, and for a moment, I stared at the portrait, the woman's eyes peering out at me from above the darkened fireplace, and I felt as if a flicker of recognition fell across her face.

I shuddered, believing that it was merely a trick of the light, but still, the face looked on. Then, I heard the creaking sound again. A series of quick clicks, like an aching door which had not been opened for a decade, slowly moving in the night. But I could not see the source. My heart raced as I looked around, and for the first time I noticed that, in the dim light, there stood an old wooden wardrobe on the other side of the room.

The creaking sounded once more; a frightful unease began to take over as each click sounded; it both puzzled and repulsed me. I turned to the door and twisted the handle as hard as I could, but the reality had not changed. I was locked in that room with a body rotting under the sheets, and a clicking noise coming from inside a wardrobe, a noise which felt alive somehow, differing itself from the shifting movements of the wooden floor and beams of the old house. It at once *sounded* so natural and now *felt and sounded* so unnatural.

Another creak, click, and I knew that I had to look in the wardrobe across the room. I was terrified by what I might find, but the anticipation of waiting, just waiting until something threatening leapt from its wooden tomb, was too much to bear. I wanted this torturous night to be over, to return to my lackluster adult life. Something had compelled me to visit my ancestral home, but I was sure that if I ever felt the cool breeze of the outside world again, I would curse this place and never return. I would let the bayou reclaim the house and bury the memories that it held within.

Obscured memories flickered in front of my eyes once more, the familiarity of the perfume stinging my senses. The room was a dreadful window into my past. I would not be tortured like this, played with; I had to know what was inside that wardrobe.

I stepped forward, moving around and then to the foot of the bed. I was certain that the portrait stared on menacingly, but I dared not catch its eye, and so my gaze remained fixed on the wardrobe as I neared it. The clicking, creaking noise sounded intermittently. With each step, I listened intently for that vile sound, other times welcoming the silence.

As I reached my hand out to the wardrobe door, I froze like a stone monument. The door moved, if ever so slightly, but it did move. I could see an inch of the darkness inside, a small sliver of black air, and I felt as though a watchful eye was glaring at me from behind the door.

I heard a creak, this time louder than before, but this sounded different, like knuckles being cracked; bone and ligament snapping, limbs which had not moved for ages, breaking free of time's relentless hold. I reached my hand out slowly and pulled the door open with force. For a moment, I thought I saw two eyes in the dark of the wardrobe watching me, but as the light from the room's singular candle reached that dark place, I saw nothing. No clothes, no belongings, no creepy eyes, just the emptiness of a life now vacant.

I sighed with relief, but when I turned to the room I froze in place. Something was different; something had changed. It wasn't the portrait above the fireplace. The bitter face of the woman in the painting continued to stare onward. It wasn't the fireplace either, remaining as it did, dark and unlit, its mouth darkened by night. It wasn't the door on the other side of the room, my only avenue for escape, standing still closed, no doubt locked by some unseen jailor wanting to incarcerate me.

No, none of these things had changed. But what had frightened me, tore at any composure I still had within me, was the figure lying under the covers in the bed. That dead, silent corpse which filled the air with perfume and macabre aura, was gone!

The red blanket had been pulled aside, revealing white silk sheets, and the only evidence that someone had been lying there was an impression in the mattress, an outline of a now missing body!

With my hand over my mouth, I gasped as the creaking sounded once more, this time from the bed, but there was no sight of the body. The room was unoccupied, and yet the air did not feel absent of company; something was there. I looked around, and it was then that I entertained a thought. One which otherwise would have been preposterous to me. Perhaps, it was an invisible specter which had been lying under the red blanket, an apparition with the body of a person, but transparent to the naked eye.

Creak.

The noise drew closer, this time from the foot of the bed. Whatever it was, it was slowly walking towards me, the warped floorboards shifting under its weight and the only sign that I wasn't alone.

If only I could see the cadaverous thing before it placed its rotten hands on me! At that thought, I leapt to the bed, and as the phantom stepped forward, I pulled the sheets off the mattress, throwing them into the air like a net. They fluttered with movement, bringing with them that sweet, rancid perfume with it. And then they came to rest, but not on the floor, instead they covered the walking corpse, showing me its outline: a shrouded dress of white sheets, resting over something hideous beneath.

Perhaps I should have allowed the thing to walk unseen. For the sight of a long-draped sheet stepping towards me almost stopped my heart. *Creak. Creak.* Each invisible footfall brought with it pangs of dread the likes of which I had never experienced before. And then came the rustling, as something else moved underneath the sheets. A reaching motion, as what I could only assume were two hands outstretched beneath their shroud reaching out towards me.

I stumbled backwards. I cried out, and as I did, the room dimmed.

My backward steps had led me into the wardrobe. The arms of the shrouded figure were now almost upon me, and my only recourse was to climb into the wardrobe and to pull the wooden doors shut, to shelter me from that thing.

My newfound sanctuary shook violently as the shrouded apparition heaved and pulled at the door. I held on with all my might, my fingers poking out into the room, grasping onto that piece of wood, the only barrier between me and that vile apparition.

Memories began to flood back, the dark wardrobe, a trigger to painful events that I had managed to bury deep within my mind. A young girl locked in darkness, dark places. Cellars, attics, wardrobes. A girl put upon, beaten, mocked. Emotionally tortured for being what she was and by her one and only caregiver. My body convulsed and shivered as the reality of my early childhood filtered through.

Suddenly, the attack ceased; the silence became deafening. And then I heard two whispered words. "Little… Susan…"

The words were more breath than voice, and in them I recognized the speaker. My grandmother. That horrid woman who had abused me, abused her duty.

"I was only a child!" I screamed at the top of

my voice. "How could you? I was confused about what I was, and you tortured and punished me for that!"

Still, I held on tightly to the door, sure that the spirit of my grandmother stood in front of it. This was confirmed to me, when I felt a warm, sticky breath on my fingers. A mouth, seen or unseen, must have hovered over them for a moment, exhaling foul air. Then, something wet licked the length of my fingers, a rotten tongue from beyond, but I dared not open the door. There was little I could do. I held onto it tightly, while the ghost of my twisted grandmother licked at my exposed flesh.

Then, nothing. Again, silence. No breath. No shaking of the doors. Nothing.

Teeth dripping with saliva suddenly bit down hard onto my fingers! I screamed in agony as they drove deep through skin and then crunched into bone. Under my screams of pain, I heard a sly smirk, a laugh of delight.

History had repeated itself as more memories flooded through the torture. She had done awful things in the past. Malevolent, twisted things. Locking me in the darkness, beating, prodding, violating me. The pain of memories mixed with the pain of the moment, as those dreaded teeth ground deeper.

"No more!"

I screamed in rage and pushed the wardrobe door open, knocking the shrouded figure to the ground. My fingers gushed blood, but they were free.

I leapt onto the bed and ran for the locked door once more. I yelled and cried and fought as the door remained tightly closed. It would not budge. I pounded and railed against my imprisonment. Then, two hands reached around me from behind, wrapping the sheet-covered fingers around my neck.

We struggled, the grip around my throat tightening, choking the breath from me. In a moment's rage and struggle, a moment of pure survival, I reached for the solitary candle which sat by the bed and cast it to the feet of my grandmother, catching the shroud of sheets ablaze. The room burned, the bed, the painting, the wardrobe. My last memory was looking beside me and seeing my grandmother's corpse burning on the floor.

I was found standing in the garden of my family home, dazed, watching it burn and collapse in on itself, watching it being consumed by flames. In the years since, I have wondered about that wraith in the room, the corpse in the bed. I had returned to my childhood home to oversee my grandmother's things after she was done with this mortal world, but it appears she was not done with me. After that night, at long last, I was certainly done with her.

BURNING JESUS

F. A. Walker

I was only four when the whole thing happened, but the memory looms large, like a movie in vivid cinematic colors. I was playing with my toys in the door of the shotgun house in which we lived, when I heard people shouting outside the house. I didn't think much of it at first: there was always something going on in town, but admittedly, we were a little far out for something to be happening there, that late.

It was suppertime. Ma was in the kitchen cooking dinner, and I remember the faint smell of sweet potatoes and hearing a sizzle, which usually meant a delicious fried something that Ma would cut up into little pieces for me. I would stick the pieces in my mouth with my hands and suck on the meat. I was playing in the doorway of the kitchen, but I was hungry, and I kept looking up at Ma, because I couldn't wait for Pa to get home, so we could eat. My sister Violet was in the highchair an arm's length away from Ma, playing in her own bowl of food, while Ma oversaw her elder's supper.

All of a sudden, I remember hearing a door slam and seeing Dad run into the kitchen, whispering feverishly. "Get the kids and go into the bedroom." As I said, we lived in a shotgun house, where one room led into another. You could see the back door from the front.

I called out, "Hi, Pa!" happy he was home early, and all he said back was, "HUSH!" in a severe tone.

I was confused at his urgency and quiet. I turned and heard a crash and the sound of breaking glass, and more shouts. Someone had hurled a brick through the front window which hit the floor, thank goodness, missing me! Then, I heard some hammering and a WHOOSH sound, and something was on fire in the front yard.

"Pa! Fire!" I was too young to be afraid, and so I was just perplexed as Papa swept me up off the floor and heaved me over his shoulder. As we went, I saw ghostly figures in white fabric with no faces and pointed heads reaching towards the sky — that, in and of itself, was scary! I could see their eyes, dark holes deep as wells cut into the fabric, with the reflection of fire shining from the slits.

"Ma, I'm scared, are those haints come to git us?" I asked. I began to feel tears running down my cheeks.

We ran towards the back room, and Pa said, "Crouch down behind the bed!" Ma had shut the fire off the evening supper and had grabbed Violet and a pot. She set the baby on the bed and filled the pot with water. I didn't know why she did that, but later, she said, if they threw a firebomb, she might need it. Then, she grabbed Violet back up and pulled me close, once Pa had set me down.

My pa had grabbed up the knife Ma had been using to cook supper and then ran to the back of the house and reached out the back door to grab the shovel. We had no gun for protection back then, as Jim Crow laws, while not expressly forbidding it, required black men in Mississippi to apply for permits. They were always denied, something that later became an issue in the 60s when Malcom X and the Black Panther Party demanded that Black folk be allowed to own guns and protect their own in times of danger. We all know how that went over.

My innocent curiosity and annoyance that my meal was going to be interrupted turned into terror when I saw through the doorways and front window the men with torches.

"Ma, why are they burning Jesus? Did he do something bad? Why are they mad?" The cross flamed in the night air, sparks jumping towards heaven.

Suddenly, a gasoline filled bottle hit the living room floor through the broken window. Pa rushed forward with a blanket to try to put it out, but the gasoline was too overpowering. He ran back to Ma, handed her the knife as he wielded the shovel, and said, "RUN! Head to the creek and follow it to Velma Rae's house. Now, RUN!"

"Orphus, I can't."

"Yes, you can! I am right behind you! Now, go!"

Ma grabbed me by the hand, and my feet flew off the floor as she did. Hugging Violet as she ran, and sending me air born, we ran into the backwoods towards the creek where I had played many times on my way to Mema and Pops' house to get cookies. But I had never been in the dark. And I had never been so filled with fear and dread.

Thankfully, my pa did follow close behind us, but both my parents turned to see their tiny house go up in flames, with Ku Klux Klan men, supposed Christians, dancing and howling like devils, as it burned.

We escaped that night, but we lost everything. That was the year Emmett Till was murdered and his killers later acquitted. The white woman who'd accused him of looking at her later admitted on her death bed that it had all been a lie.

I am an old man now, and the whole thing makes me sad, our history, but I'll never forget that terrifying feeling I experienced that night or the sickness in my heart and the fear in my stomach that I'd felt. I didn't know then, but that was the feeling of my innocence dying, while a doubt and mistrust of mankind was newly born.

WHERE DID THE DINOSAURS GO?

Kristina Lee

Calissa wiped her brow with a lacy handkerchief. The weather was very humid in the jungle where she found herself. Calissa had jobs like this before, where she was soaked to the skin, broiling in the sun's punishing rays. Going for the water bottle to drench herself in cool cleansing liquid was a blessing. She had her faith to keep her company all the way out here, in the Amazon.

"Saint Helena, please watch over me in this time fraught with problems and distractions."

The main distraction was the six-foot three tall blond god named Cael who worked opposite Calissa. She might have completed her work by now, if there hadn't been shutdowns of the site due to superstitions by local guides. The superstitions were whispered fervently by all the native people who worked clearing the rocks from the blast. The whispers were in their native tongue of Tupian, also called Tupari. *Noo Dako nay, Anoa eYi*, roughly translated to "Other Lizard Tooth" and "Heart Blood."

Some people working with Calissa had gone missing. One minute, they were there, and the next, they were not. Maybe the superstitions had gotten to them, and they ran off.

The men digging called to her that they had found something. Calissa ran to the site and saw purple crystals unlike any she had seen before. She ran her hand over them, and they hummed and vibrated.

Her friend Cael snatched her hand away.

"Don't touch them! We don't know their origin!"

Calissa abruptly stood up, wrenching her hand from Cael's.

"You have never seen anything like it, either."

Cael said, "No, I haven't. What kind of archaeologist touches an artifact with his ungloved hands?" He stormed off.

A worker came stumbling towards Calissa, holding his neck, which was bleeding.

"MFFmmff,"

Calissa asked, "What are you trying to say?! Quick, let me staunch the blood flow!" Calissa tore a strip of cotton from her shirt and applied it to the man's neck with pressure. She made a bandage out of leaves and cotton from her shirt. Once the wound was dressed, she asked the worker what happened to him.

He answered, "*Noo Dako nay, Anoa eYi.*"

"What happened to your neck?" she asked again, as she gestured to try and make herself clearer.

Calissa laid the man down gently and thought to herself that she didn't recognize this worker, and she knew most of them. She wondered who the man was and whether he would remain stable out here in the wild. He was okay now, but what if gangrene set in? Then he could go septic. There was a doctor in the neighboring village, but they would need a guide to take them there. The neighboring village was 160 kilometers away.

Calissa signed to the workers with which she was familiar. She called them Bob and Dave, because their names were so hard to pronounce in Tupari. She asked them to take the unidentified man to the neighboring village and leave him with the shaman/doctor. Bob and Dave set off in a northerly direction, and Calissa prayed for the man to pull through or to be at peace, whichever God wanted.

Calissa was concerned for the injured man, but they were on a deadline, so she had to get back to work. Where were the helpers? *Sigh.* They must have thought to take a break, since she stopped earlier to deal with the strange man.

Calissa bent down to observe the purple crystals. Then, she put on her gloves and examined the crystals with her hands. The vibration was constant; it made her hands warm.

Later, in the camp bath tent, Calissa looked in the mirror after having taken a good scrub in the shower. Her wet hair curled at her nape. She thought she saw something in the reflection of the doorway. She turned.

"Anybody there?" She clutched the towel closer to her and looked behind her. No one was there. She went back to finger combing her fiery hair. There it was again. Calissa was getting a spooky feeling and goosebumps on her bare skin.

All of a sudden, she saw a reptile squatting in the tent doorway. Calissa blinked a couple of times, but the image stayed the same. The creature started moving towards her, teeth visible, dripping with saliva.

Calissa slowly moved backward. Then, when she couldn't stand it anymore, she made a break for it and made a beeline for the door behind her.

She ran out into daylight and into the arms of Cael. He slowed her sprint and was saying something to her, but she didn't respond. Only then did she realize she was only in a skimpy towel, and all the workers were looking at her. Calissa looked around at all the eyes, and now that she was in the sunshine, she thought the reptile may have been nothing but a daydream, more like a day-mare.

Cael was still saying something to her. "Are you hurt? You are shivering ferociously!" He looked into her eyes and couldn't help noticing the curves that were hardly covered by that thin cloth.

Calissa finally came out of shock and heard what Cael had been shouting at her.

"Are you okay?

Calissa answered, "Yes, I am okay. I was just startled by something that I saw in the mirror. Turned out, it was nothing."

Cael said, "Are you sure? You're still shaking."

"Yes, Cael, I'm okay." Calissa looked down again, blushing profusely. She needed to get out of this towel and into some clothes. "Excuse me."

Calissa went back to her tent and dressed for the evening heat. Cael watched her walk away. He felt a peculiar feeling in his stomach that he had never felt before with any other woman.

Just then, the worker Calissa had patched up came shambling into camp with the makeshift bandage she had applied earlier. Calissa wondered what he was doing there. The worker threw punches at two other guys taking a break and bulldozed right to the site. She noticed he was going right for the crystals, but why? Cael tried to stop the worker, but the worker punched him, too! The man had to have incredible strength to knock Cael out. Suddenly, the worker made off with the purple crystals and vanished into the jungle!

When Cael came to an hour later, he said, "What was that guy on? He was super strong!"

Calissa replaced the wet washcloth on Cael's head and eased him back down. He had quite a bump on the back of his head.

"Cael, are you okay? You took a big hit!"

He replied, "Yeah, I'm fine." Cael scratched his head, then winced and said, "Aww!"

Calissa said, "See, you are not all right! You just shouted out in pain. I will be staying with you tonight, so I can make sure you don't have a concussion."

As she settled down for the night, Calissa knew she had a monumental task ahead of her: to keep an eye on Cael (and not seduce him!) while he was lying in his sleeping bag not two feet to her right in her tent.

All of a sudden, the wind howled, and the tent was nearly ripped out from its stakes. Worse than that, they heard a creature approaching! Calissa thought, *Oh no, it can't be!* That same reptile she had seen—not imagined!—ripped through the tent, reaching out for Cael! All Calissa could hear was the screeching Cael was emitting next to her. He was injured by the reptile and was trying to fend off another attack, while trying to staunch the wound.

Calissa started to pray to Helena over and over. Finally, when she opened her eyes, the battle was over. The reptile was gone.

Cael was bleeding pretty badly, but he would live. Once again, Calissa dressed his wounds, and they both tried to get some sleep, but she kept thinking how she had been praying and that the monster went away. Had her prayers saved them?

The reptile must have been a demon. Most likely, this was the thing that attacked that worker. It must have infected him with its unholy essence. They were all alone in the jungle with the potential of unholy beasts, and their only weapon was prayer. Calissa prayed over Cael to make sure he didn't become one of them.

She knew the crystals must have something to do with the arrival of the reptiles. There were more than likely others than that just one. They needed to find more crystals. Maybe that was the key to this mystery.

After a couple of days and no more attacks, Calissa and Cael ventured back to the dig site and spent hours painstakingly brushing the soil.

Calissa wiped her brow after stooping for so

long. She stretched her back, and Cael drank some water out of his canteen. He looked pale. He needed to rest, but he insisted on helping. Once they had taken a break, they began toiling again.

Just as they were about to give up, Cael getting weaker, Calissa saw a glowing purple in the dirt. They uncovered the purple crystal and a tablet that was inscribed in Tupari. Calissa translated it, and it said, "The sharp tooth must be killed. The only way is to hurt the crystal."

Calissa looked up, and she saw a reptile surprisingly similar to a *T-Rex*. Then, she looked slightly to the right and saw another one, then another! They were surrounded by them!

Calissa hugged Cael close to her, and they remembered what the tablet had said: to break the crystals with a chisel. They quickly demolished the crystals, with hammers and chisels, their beauty now smashed to bits. As they did so, the "dinosaurs" vanished like a puff of smoke! The duo were in each other's arms, and Cael reached down to Calissa's chin, lifted it up and kissed her.

Where did the dinosaurs go? Some say a meteor came and killed them all; others say climate change. I say, it was a trans-dimensional phenomenon. The dinosaurs simply went to another dimension and can be seen now and again through portals like doorways, and sometimes they can come back through the portals. They are drawn to the crystals that Calissa and Cael had unearthed that day in the jungle.

.

ENTICED IN THE DARKNESS

Bernadette Lowe

It was that perfect evening when teens gathered, nothing to do; a time when every dream, every wish, every thought can come true, as though magical.

Dusk, that enchanted time of night, was offset by the golden orange mist that spread across the sky as the sun set in the west, leaving shoots of sunrays that intermixed with the hues of the sky. Softened by a purple haze, the orange glow seemed to penetrate the sprinkling of soft, white pillows of clouds. It was one of those memorable sunsets, filled with dramatic color, perfect for the young of heart who gathered to venture forth.

Perched on a tailgate and chairs, they watched the sky diminish into the darkness of the night, watching the moon enter their vision, pop into full view, lighting up the night with just a hint of a romantic soft glow that beckoned as if to say, "Come, dance with me. I await your presence."

"Why don't we take a moonlight drive?" asked Tobi.

"How 'bout skinny dipping? Dare ya!" exclaimed Josh, the adventurous type, who was always ready for the unexpected.

The soft-spoken angelic looking girl, Julie, was beautiful with golden blonde hair. With a twinkle in her eye, she merely tossed her hair, smiled, and gently coaxed, "Would you really like to be dared?"

Karen, her best friend, smiled inwardly, knowing that this just might be a night to never forget. She listened as Julie continued verbally edging everyone forward.

Julie was always charming, enticing, and now she was chanting, "I know the perfect place for a chase. Game on!"

Dashing, she ran, never looking behind, knowing full well that her entourage would follow, meekly, like lambs, for she had brilliant ideas that were always, later, the spark of conversation.

And so it was that a car and pick-up full of teens headed for a night of adventure, a night of chase and daring. Julie knew where they were headed. She drove her car, loaded and packed with teens, heading into the dark of downtown, where the day's activities had long ago been drowned out with the dimming of the sun. The skyline was filled with silent tall, dark buildings, and the whispering of the empty streets, highlighted with a splash of the golden moonshine hit the tips of the dark, empty buildings with an eerie cast, a foreboding of the night to be.

Once, it was an elegant building, now abandoned. Eleven stories high, it graced the landscape with two castle-like inset rounded towers, perched between three brick stacks of the century-old prestigious hotel. Jutted on top of the roofline were narrow columns that almost reached the sky, complete with corbels and decorative stone, giving a hint of the small secret buildings on top of the massive hotel.

Parking, Julie exited her vehicle, smiled at Tom, her boyfriend, grabbed his hand, then gathered the troops and pointed, smiling,

"A tire iron, and we're in. There's no one there, and we all have flashlights on our phones. Party time! Let's split in two groups. The first one to find a bar of old soap and an initialed towel heads to the lobby. First group there, wins!"

Josh grabbed the tire iron, hit the glass as the sound reverberated and bounced off ceilings and walls, echoing and re-echoing. Raking the edges clean, he maneuvered his lean, muscled body inside, forming the entry path for others who watched in disbelief, unable to comprehend that they were a party to this out-of-control event. And yet, teen-like, they followed, each choking their silent regret, unable to voice their dissent.

Flashing their lights, they entered, for the first

time ever, seeing the stark, naked black of the inside, the remnants of society's greatest elegance. Brushing aside a galore of spider webs, the guys went first, followed by the girls.

"Nasty, ooooh," spoke Karen, who was very delicate and despised spiders with a passion.

Like the others, she could not believe they were partaking in such an event which held them all spellbound, all with the same initiative – to find the damn soap and towel and depart the freaky event. Not a one thought of speaking his or her mind and standing up to Julie, the soft-spoken, carefully measured talking, hell-bound leader.

Huge columns extended twenty feet tall, with all the nuance that softly whispered to all the elite and prestigious former visitors. Layers of exquisite hand-carved crown molding displayed ornate leaves, carefully etched to withstand the grains of time. The old elevators, no longer brought to life, sat open, displaying the chair of the operator, going nowhere, just waiting.

Every footstep brought forth a creak, a groan, a hint of mystery, excitement, fear, and anxiety. Amy was terrified, in over her head, with no graceful way to back down, to undo what she had done. She clung close to her boyfriend, Sam, following his lead. Sam, of course, was not about to tell Amy that he, also, was in way over his head. He just wanted to quickly find the objects and leave the damn place and never return. His regrets bounced inside his head as his eyes adjusted, somewhat, to the blackness of night.

Julie was on a high, for she felt no fear, ever. Always in control, no matter the twists and turns, she had the advantage, a way with words, and gracefully, could charm the knickers off a nun with no effort. Dashing forth, she felt Tom's soft breath as he neared, his lips brushing her neckline, softly whispering, "Oh baby, we're alone."

With a brush of her hand, she escaped from her boyfriend, happily skipping from crook to cranny, feeling her way forward, searching for a bathroom. She knew Tom was behind her, even though she no longer felt the spray of his light. Hearing an echo of a nearby unrecognized sound, cognizant, she turned slightly, feeling him grasp her by the arm, spin her around, forcefully pushing her into the wall.

Her head was reeling as she sucked in a breath and smelled the stench of rotten from his teeth. Every bone in her body was screaming that something was bad wrong. Tom was gentle, and his smell was romantically enticing, not rotten.

Her flashlight fell to the ground, displaying light that was pooled in the distance, with little reflection near her. She saw the silhouette of his hood-covered face, the two eyes penetrating her eyes, as she screamed a 4th floor scream that couldn't be heard by other floors. She saw the flash of the edge of the knife blade. Wrestling, trying to maneuver from this stranger of darkness, she felt the sting of something in her forearm, saw the hypodermic needle, and knew she was in over her head.

"If you scream again, I'll kill you!" she heard her determined attacker softly say, and Julie realized that this man was in control of this situation, feeling him fumbling and grasping with her clothes.

Terrified, silenced, she slumped downward, feeling the call of the sandman, way too early in the night, way too fast. She tried to force her hands to stretch outward, to find her cell phone.

"Focus, focus," she repeatedly told herself, following the ray of light, hopefully to find the inception of the beam, but her eyes kept closing, the lids becoming harder to open.

She could feel the arm shaking her, hear the voice, but she was too groggy to fully understand. Soaking wet, sweating, terrified, moving a hand, grasping, with effort, she tried to find the damn flashlight as the arm continued shaking her. She was terrified, couldn't hear her voice but felt her vocal cords contracting, trying to scream.

And then it happened.

The damn TV emergency alert sounded.
She woke up.

Beware of what you watch on TV. It might visit you in the middle of the night!

STAY AWAY FROM THE PLATT PLACE

Julie Marquardt

Farm country, southern Wisconsin, 1934 - two years before electricity would come to the area. This is where and when the epic tale of the exploration of the Platt place, an abandoned farmhouse sitting silent and empty for years, occurred.

"Stay away from the Platt place...it's haunted," the grown-ups told all the kids. No one was quite sure who or what was haunting the abandoned house, but when the grown-ups said something, it was taken as gospel...mostly.

The words "stay away" were probably the biggest challenge ever heard by every little boy around. Three boys, in particular, found the possibility of discovering what the mystery of the house was, to be too compelling to ignore. This decision was not made lightly. In those days, kids did what they were told, and few, if any, questions were asked.

At school, the boys, Earl and Wesley, inexperienced first graders who faithfully followed Earl's brother, Art, older and more worldly in the second grade, talked about a daring plan. They agreed to meet up at the old farmhouse the next day,

Saturday, to explore every room in the scary old house and find out just what the story was. The bragging rights alone would be worth any fear they might feel at the thought of disobeying or the possibility of actually finding ghosts. They'd prove the grown-ups wrong, because after their exploration, they were sure the mystery would be solved, the mystery everyone else was afraid to investigate. Surely, they would be considered heroes when they succeeded in their mission and told everyone what they had done and, more importantly, what they discovered.

Arriving at the agreed upon time, they immediately saw the front porch, uncovered and exposed to the elements, was completely rotted, and they had to step very carefully even to get to the gaping front door. Adding to the forlorn appearance, all the windows were broken out.

Stepping through the doorway into the front room, they found they could see pretty well. Bright light from the open door and broken windows spilled into the room, allowing them to see into the still emptiness. The quiet didn't faze the intrepid explorers one bit, and they walked bravely into the shadowy space, staying together.

Somewhat to their disappointment, as they

walked through the downstairs rooms, they soon discovered there was nothing in the house, nothing at all! No old furniture, draperies, rugs, no bits and pieces of the lives of the people who had once lived here and had once called this place home. It made the emptiness feel spookier somehow. The boys glanced at each other reassuringly, bolstering their courage.

There was not much conversation, other than an occasional "Nothing here," as they searched. Having found no ghosts on the first floor, they made their way silently up the wooden staircase to the three rooms upstairs.

By this point, they had pretty much determined that the old Platt place was just a house - a normal, old farmhouse much like the boys' own houses. Had the grown-ups maybe made up the stories about it being haunted? They were all witness to the fact that there were no ghosts, scary or otherwise, living here.

Still staying together - because more witnesses was better, right? - they completed their search, checking all the rooms. They finished quickly, since closets weren't even built into houses then, so it wasn't hard to see that, as with the main floor, every room was starkly bare.

There was just one more place to look for the elusive ghosts, so they tromped back down the stairs. In truth, by now the quest was more about being thorough and just seeing what was there, rather than seeking apparitions from the beyond.

Near the front entrance was the only door that had not yet been opened, the one they'd saved for last. They knew this one led to the root cellar, a familiar site in or around every old home. There would be stairs going down to a small space dug into the ground, where foodstuffs were stored on shelves and kept cool. They opened the door and, not giving it a second thought, started down the stairs, not really considering how they'd be able to explore the pitch-black cavern below with no hint of light to help them see. Turns out they didn't need any help to see what was before them.

Peering down into the darkness, to their utter horror and dismay, two bright, shining eyes stared back up at them from the bottom of the stairs. Hearts pounding, they were too terrified even to register the color of the gleaming, unblinking eyes of the ghost. The warnings were true - the old Platt place *was* haunted!

No words were needed. There were no shouts of "Run!" - no girly screams - not even any manly screams, nothing but gasps of terror and the thundering of feet as all three explorers turned as one and high-tailed it back up the stairs and towards the still open front door. It was every man for himself.

The only sounds were the thumping of shoes on the wooden floors. And the rotten porch? What porch? Three small bodies flew through the air as three pairs of feet sailed over the entire expanse, not one foot touching a single rotten board. Their solid landings in the dirt beyond were gold medal worthy; no stumbling, no hesitation. Not a word was spoken - again, there was no need, every man knew what needed to be done and did it.

Feet on the ground, Wesley turned west towards his home, and the brothers shot straight ahead to the farm where they lived, not stopping for anything until they reached the fence line between properties. They were amazed at how fast they could run. Their fear made them race like the wind.

Scooting under the barbed wire fence and figuring they were safe, the two boys took a moment to look back for Wesley. Seeing no sign of him and feeling certain he, too, had made it to safety, they continued across the pasture towards home.

Not much was ever said again about the infamous expedition. First off, they couldn't exactly brag about having disobeyed the orders to keep away; now, could they? Certainly not with their sorry results. And second, no one was exactly proud of their mindlessly terrified flight from the danger. Nope, no one ever needed to know there were no heroes at the Platt place that day.

DON'T KNOCK, JUST RUN

Les McDermott

The beautiful brick columns with iron gates showed the way to a curved driveway to a small two-story house. too small for a mansion, but bigger than any house in the town. The manicured yard and flowers around the walkway brought out the beauty of the front of the house.

This was fifty years ago; now. Tt was overgrown with weed and trees, and the gates were almost ready to fall. Some of the brick on the columns had fallen out, and the house looked haunted. This was the greatest place on earth, was the thinking of teenagers through the past few years. The story went that no one knew who had lived there, and then, one day, someone noticed no one was living there.

The sheriff went through the house and found no one, and it looked like no one had ever lived there. The court records showed that a man and wife, named Mr. and Mrs. Abbot, had owned the house, but where were they? Records showed that a corporation paid the taxes, and none could be traced any farther back. So, the house just stayed empty, and one day the sheriff chained up the gates to keep kids out.

For the past several years, it was left alone, just to deteriorate, yet the kids continually snuck in. Some broke things, but most just explored the old house. Someone started rumors for the fun of it, and of course, things got out of hand, and now all the stories of the haunted house appeared true.

One late summer evening with a partial moon out, little Johnny and Mary decided to go out to the old place, and you know, explore. At the gate, like all the other times, they pulled the bottom of the gate out and slipped through. Johnny and Mary, giggling, walked up the driveway, looking around for anyone or things. The gentle breeze through the trees and the swaying of the tall grass and weeds did make it eerie. The light from the moon just made it much scarier.

Flickering moonlight coming through made long shadows of the tree limbs. They looked like arms reaching out to get you. Johnny and Mary giggled from being scared, but curiosity drove them on. Being alone was on their minds; the closer they got to the house, the more nervous they got. They approached the front door, and it was partially open.

The dirt on the entry way has been there for some time. "No tracks going in," Johnny said, figuring no one else was here.

"Is that good?" asked Mary, as she grabbed and

pulled him to her. As Mary wrapped her leg around Johnny, he got the idea quick.

They started taking each other's clothes off.

Johnny said, "What if the ghosts are watching?"

"Let 'em watch! They need a little excitement on the other side."

Just when they got naked, a loud rumbling noise started coming toward them and was getting louder. They jumped up, grabbing their clothes and, dropping some, they ran to the door.

The door slammed shut, just before they got there. Johnny tried to open it, but it was locked! He looked around and saw the window and raised it up and jumped out, turning to help Mary. He got a face full of clothes as she jumped out the window. They picked up their clothes and ran to the gate, dropping more pieces of clothing.

Mary said, "This had better not be any of your friends doing this," still trying to put some clothing on.

"No one knew we were coming out here," said Johnny, as he pulled the bottom of the gate back, allowing Mary to slip through it like greased lightning, and he was close behind. They were still trying to put on their clothes and trying to get into his pickup, when red lights came on, and a siren blasted at them.

"Oh no," said Johnny. "It's Deputy Dog."

A large fat man of 300 pounds appeared, who the kids had nicknamed, because of how funny he was when he chased them. His police belt had keys dangling from it and loosely fit around him, flopping up and down when he ran--or tried to. In this small town, they teased him, but they liked him anyway.

"All right, kids, were you in the old Abbot place?" Deputy Dog asked.

"Yea," said Johnny, still trying to catch his breath.

Deputy Ralph shined his flashlight on Mary, to see who the other person was. "You know the trouble you can get into, and I don't mean the law," said the deputy.

Both kids started talking at the same time, telling what happened to them. Ralph knew the kids had been in there before, and nothing had ever happened. Curious, he started looking around at the place, spotting his flashlight at the house and around the yard.

"Seriously," said Johnny, "the door locked on us, and a loud noise was coming at us, and we couldn't see anything. I opened the window for us to get out, and I left it open."

Deputy Ralph wasn't sure he believed them, so Johnny said, "Go inside and see for yourself."

"No, better wait for tomorrow," said Deputy Ralph.

"You afraid, Deputy?" asked Johnny.

Deputy Ralph thought, *What a smart ass, to pressure me to go inside tonight.*

"Dang it, police officers are not afraid of anything," said the Deputy. "I need you to hold the gate open, so I can get through." Ralph got down on all fours, and Johnny pulled back on the gate, "Farther," said Ralph.

Johnny said, "I can't move it anymore."

Then, Ralph realized he was stuck. "Get me out of here, boy. You did this on purpose."

"No, no, I didn't," said Johnny, trying not to laugh. "Mary, get the rope out of the toolbox and hook it on the gate, and I'll pull the pickup around to pull the gate open," said Johnny.

"Hook it on the gate, not me," hollered Deputy Ralph, "and pull really easy." At about that time, the whole gate came crashing down on top of the deputy.

Johnny walked up to Ralph sitting on the ground and said, "You can go in now."

The deputy got up and gave the evil eye to Johnny and said, "Don't leave while I'm in there."

Walking up the driveway was just like the kids earlier: the gentle breeze through the trees and the tall grasses and weeds swaying and the moonlight causing shadows on everything.

The house looked like it always had to him. He hollered back at the kids, "Did anybody lose some panties or socks? What, no answer? That's what I expected," said the deputy, mumbling.

When he got to the front steps, he noticed the front door was partially open, and the dust on the entry hadn't been disturbed. That was not what Johnny said, and the window was closed, not open or broken. *So, what were these kids up to?* he wondered, as he walked on into the first room.

There was old trash lying around and stuff you didn't want to pick up. A couple of more steps and as Ralph reached in the middle of the room, the door slammed shut! Turning faster than he had ever moved before, Deputy Dog was sweating like rain by now. Noises were moving toward him, and he grabbed his gun, but something grabbed *him*, instead!

Johnny and Mary were standing at the gate, not wanting to go in, but watching for Deputy Dog to come back out. Then, the expected--or unexpected — happened. They heard the deputy yell and start screaming. They looked at each other and ran and jumped into Johnny's pickup.

Of course, it wouldn't start! He tried again. It

wouldn't start, and then a big bang, and the pickup bounced. The two kids looked at each other, more scared than ever before.

Johnny tried again, and the pickup started, and he slammed it into gear and took off. Mary hollered out the window, "Ralph, you're on your own! We'll get help!"

They got to the police department in no time at all, and Johnny locked the brakes up and slid into the parking area and jumped out. The door of the police office flew open and surprised the only other cop on duty. Johnny was breathing hard, and Mary was hanging onto him. Neither could talk, but finally, the officer got something out that made sense.

"Deputy Dog is in trouble, Doc!"

Doc was a retired medical examiner and police chief, and he knew these kids weren't kidding.

"What's going on, and where is Ralph?" said Doc.

"At the Abbot place. We left him when we heard screaming and yelling," said Mary.

"That was kind of you, leaving him alone," said Doc.

"What could we do, and my pickup wouldn't start. Then, something hit us," said Johnny.

"Let's go see what hit you," said Doc, not sure what to believe. He ran his hand on the top side of the truck bed, which was kinda high, because all the kids in town jacked up their trucks. Doc stopped and got a cold chill running down his back, when a hand grabbed him.

Johnny and Mary jumped back against a police car, which must have moved them two feet, before they froze.

Moaning, Deputy Ralph sat up, holding his head. Looking at them, he said, "How did I get here?"

Johnny said, "I drove here."

"No, I mean, how did I get in your truck?"

Surprised by all this, Doc could only say, "I think we need to wait for morning to see what's going on."

THE LADDER AND THE HAMSTER WHEEL

Andrea Foster

George had heard the noises all night and had tossed and turned listening to them. They were squeaks, some animal, some machine-like—there had been both, and since he had to get up early the next day, he had tried to force himself to sleep that night, despite the odd noises. He fretted over whether he should call the neighborhood watch or the police, but he didn't want to get in a bad way with the neighbors, so he listened to the eekeekeek all night long and slept fitfully.

In the morning, he dragged himself straight off to work, walking by the huge ivied wall, wondering what on earth could be making such an irritating noise, ceaselessly, for all those hours. When he came home that day, the squeaking and squealing had stopped. He was still exhausted from lack of sleep, but since no one was around, he decided to have a look over the wall.

Wouldn't ya know, he then spied a ladder lying on the ground nearby and pulled it up to the huge fence. Up the ladder he climbed and stood silently, surveying the scene.

He had never seen over that wall in all the

years he had lived next door. He had never noticed anybody doing much of anything over there. From what he knew, there was an old lady who lived there that never came out of her cottage. He had heard that she was sick and that her granddaughter visited on occasion to help out.

Now, as he looked over the fence, he saw a huge contraption that looked like a hamster wheel, only much bigger. As he looked over the fence, he saw eyes at the window; someone had seen him! Suddenly, there was a woman in the yard, and she came right over and looked up at him.

"Who are YOU?" she asked, surprisingly friendly. She lowered her eyes, in what looked like a slight flirtation.

"I am George Hadley," George said, shy and embarrassed to be caught snooping on another person's life.

"Well, hello, George Hadley! I see you have been looking at my wheel. This wheel helps me to help my mother. She is out of sorts, and if I hook her up to this wheel, I can help her get some of her energy back. She's a bit pallid, you see. Needs exercise."

George tried to imagine an old lady in the hamster wheel—or even the younger woman in the contraption. He saw all kinds of tubes and pullies hooked up to the wheel, going in through the window.

"Would you like to come have some tea and get a closer look?" The woman raised her skirt a little in that old-fashioned, hitchhiking pose he'd seen actresses use in black and white movies.

George blushed, because no woman had ever flirted with him and wasn't ever likely to again, so he gulped and stammered, "Y-yes!"

"Here, let me put a ladder on this side." The woman already had a nice ladder, as tall or taller than his, and she placed it on her side, near him. George climbed over the fence with an agility he hadn't known he still had. He was eager to have tea with a lovely lady. He felt guilty for thinking how he wished the old lady would die, so the younger one could move in. He shook off such a thought and alighted on the other side of the fence. He bowed and removed his hat and held out his hand.

The woman took his hand and squeezed it; she was rather strong for a woman, he thought. She did not let go.

"Want to see my machine?" she asked, stepping into the wheel, and he heard its squeak. He knew that's what he had heard last night. Was she the one who had made that contraption squeak with that awful sound all night long last night? Was she the one whimpering and squealing? Weird!

He stepped into the wheel with her, as she had not released his hand, and she leaned into him in the most pleasurable way. He blushed. She felt his face with one of her hands. Her other hand was around his waist. He felt light-headed, happy, delighted.

Just as he was coming to his senses, the woman suddenly stuffed a wad of cloth into his mouth, swiftly latching a belt around his head. He had been muzzled! He didn't know yet if this was meant to be fun or shocking.

The young woman laughed. He had heard of women like this. She turned away from him for a second and then jabbed him with a needle-like implement, and blood spurted.

Oh, no, this wasn't fun. He started to struggle with her, but she was quick. She leapt from the machine, hit a lever, and he heard a huge BAM and found himself caged.

He was still spurting blood, and she said, "Give me your arm, and I'll stop the bleeding." She sounded so sweet. He held out his arm. She tied a tourniquet on the arm, and then somehow hooked him up to a tube. She was taking his blood! He saw her adjusting the tubes through the window, and then, she disappeared into the house.

He heard her say, "There, there, Mother, we'll

get you some fresh blood, and you'll be as good as new!" She started to hum a jaunty tune.

In a minute, she returned and stood watching him and said, "Now, WALK, MAN! WALK."

George started walking, and the hamster wheel began to rotate and squeak, just like he'd heard the night before. He tried to talk, but all he could do was squeal.

"Now, you do well, honey, and I'll give you a rest." George trudged, squeaking and squealing. The lady went back inside the house.

Later, after the lady had kept her promise, she removed his body with help of a big garden cart and her mother's pet goat. George Hadley got his rest. She laid him to rest in the garden under a big walnut tree.

She could hear someone walking by, going, "Wonder what's inside the fence...Look! A ladder! I think I'll look!" The lady smiled.

THE CREATURE FROM THE DARK

JoJo Maize

On that summer day in 1970, I was visiting my friend, Jerry, at his house. Several of us thirteen-year-olds, were hanging around his home, along with a couple of twelve-year-olds.

It had been a typical summer day in small town America. This particular town had only one traffic light, and if that doesn't paint a picture, let's just say the sidewalks rolled-up when the sun went down. It was a sleepy little community in which nothing exciting ever happened.

The street in front of Jerry's house had had all the old paving removed, in preparation for new pavement. His street was nothing more than a dirt road.

We were sitting on his front porch like statues, trying to stay cool in the oppressive heat. That's when we heard a loud engine coming down the street. It was a water tanker spraying water in a wide arc out the back to wet the dirt and keep the dust down. Those of us with bicycles jumped on them and followed along behind the truck enjoying the concentrated and dense spray of water.

Once the truck operator turned off the spray,

there was nothing left to do but go back to sitting on Jerry's porch.

Tim said, "Gosh, it's so hot, I feel like I'm drowning."

Jerry frowned and asked, "What the heck is that supposed to mean?"

"I don't know," Tim said. "It's something my Dad says when it's boiling outside."

We all took turns joshing Tim about how grown up he sounded and then went back to being hot and bored.

As the sun began to head toward the western horizon, Jeff asked, "What time is it?"

"It's almost seven-thirty," I said.

"Oh, crap! I'm supposed to be home before it gets dark." Jeff whined. "It'll take me at least twenty minutes to walk. I'm gonna have to run all the way," anxiety dripping off him like the sweat down my back.

"Come on. I'll give you a ride," I said. I had a Schwinn bicycle with a banana seat and a sissy bar on the back. I had just bought it from a local thrift shop with the money I made mowing lawns. I could quickly get him home in just a matter of minutes.

We charged out of the yard, me pretending I was the hero of the day. Like the Green Hornet. Or Batman in his Batmobile. We raced down E Street and took a right on Eighth Street. I forgot there would be a lip from the unpaved E Street back up onto the paved Eighth Street and so nearly lost Jeff at the bump. Would have, too, if not for the sissy bar.

We were heading, fast toward, the lumber yard when we both saw it. It ran across the road in front of us. It ran north from the small gravel pit, across Eighth, and into the large lumber warehouse.

I slammed on my brake, skidding to a halt. I stood there for half a beat before Jeff, still sitting on the seat, began to pound on my back, "Get out of here!"

I was stunned and shaking, but I stood on the pedals and quickly made a U-turn in the middle of the street. I don't remember the ride back. I do remember when we got back to Jerry's, most of the kids had left. Jerry was sitting on the porch with his older sister, Natalie, and one or two other boys.

I guess they could tell something wasn't right. "What are you guys doing back here?" Jerry asked.

I'll be the first to admit that I was freaking out. Jeff wasn't doing much better when we tried to tell them what we had witnessed. We hadn't discussed what we had seen; we had been too busy getting back without crashing the bike. But our stories were identical.

The creature was big, tall, and hairy. And fast.

We were so afraid it may have followed us, we insisted we go in the house and lock the doors. Natalie, Jerry's sister, at first thought we were making it up, but I guess she could tell by our faces and the fear in our eyes we were serious. Natalie called the police.

Jeff called his parents and asked them to come. He told them something had happened, and the police were on their way. I couldn't hear the other end of the conversation, but suddenly Jeff took the telephone from his ear, looked at the phone like it was from another planet, and screamed, "Just come!" Then he slammed the phone down, and we all stood in a circle staring at each other, not knowing what to do next.

A police car pulled in the driveway, and we ran out to the porch. We all knew Sergeant Jansen, so Jeff and I jumped right into our story at the same time, making no sense, I'm sure. As another police officer parked in front of the house, Sergeant Jansen told Jeff to stand at the other end of the porch. He then told the second officer, who turned out to be Officer Sanger, to get Jeff's story.

"Okay," Sergeant Jansen said to me, "What did you see?"

I took a calming breath and began to tell him about the dark shape, covered in fur, running across the street in front of us like a man. "But it was really, really tall," I told him.

Sergeant Jansen asked, "How tall would you say it was?"

I looked around for something I could relate to the height of the monster I had seen. I pointed at the frame of the front door on the house and said, "That tall."

Jeff and Officer Sanger heard my description of the height, and Jeff said, "Yeah! That's about how tall! That thing was huge!"

Jeff's parents showed up and went to Jeff. He and Officer Sanger were catching them up on the commotion. I couldn't hear what Jeff was telling them, but when he finished, both the officers and Jeff's parents went down the front steps and out to one of the cars. They stood around talking for a little bit, then came back up to speak to us again.

That's when the radios in their cars began to squawk. Another officer was screaming into his radio about seeing a creature running down an alley. He said the animal had jumped a fence into a backyard. The two officers jumped in their cars and, yelling at us to stay put, took off.

Jeff's parents took him home, but I could tell he wanted to stay with me. We had a shared experience that bonded us. I felt like they were taking my only brother from me. And I'm an only child!

An hour or so went by with us waiting for the police officers to return. I called my mom to tell her what was happening, but she didn't answer the phone.

When Officer Sanger came back, he said he didn't know what we had seen. He felt like it was probably some hobo off the nearby tracks. For some reason, I chose not to contradict him.

I was suddenly so tired; I just wanted to go home and go to bed. I got on my bike and headed toward home, being on high alert all the way. I couldn't stop feeling like I was being watched or followed.

It was nearly 10 o'clock and full-on dark outside. I was feeling mighty grateful for street-lights. As I turned onto Fig Avenue, I realized the streetlights were out on that street. I was already on edge, so it didn't take much to spook me.

I stopped at the head of the street, trying to think of another way to get home. I seriously did not want to drive into the dark.

Don't be stupid. You've ridden down this street a thousand times. Just get it over with, I thought. I told myself I knew every inch of that street, where all the potholes were, and which corners had stop signs. I could ride down that street and be home in just a few minutes.

I took off down the street, not riding too fast or too slow, trying to convince myself there was nothing to fear.

Suddenly, out of the corner of my eye, I saw a massive beast charging out at me from between two houses, barking, its jaws slavering, and biting at my heels.

I raced away as fast as I could ride until the big dog gave up and turned back toward its home.

"Stupid dog," I muttered, just before my front tire landed in one of those darn potholes. I took flight, somersaulting over the handlebars, landing hard on my back, my head glancing off the pavement.

I lay there stunned for a moment. Out of the dark, and even more massive than the massive dog, a creature crouched over me. I froze. My mind was trying to remember what you're supposed to do when confronted by a bear. That was when the creature grabbed me with its hands. *Hands? Bears don't have hands,* I thought.

The creature lifted me and stood me on my feet. She brushed me off (yes, it was definitely a "she") and began sniffing my hair. Then, she licked the top of my head before running off into the dark.

My house was dark when I arrived home.

Mom wasn't around. I bolted the door and went to the kitchen to make myself a sandwich, which I took to my room in the attic. I scarfed down my dinner and passed out on my bed.

The next morning, I ran downstairs to tell my mom about the creature.

"Mom! Mom," I yelled as I clamored down the stairs.

My mom was sitting at the little table in the kitchen smoking a cigarette and drinking her coffee when she said, "Oh, for God's sake, Lonnie. Keep it down. I've got a splitting headache."

I looked at her accusingly and asked, "Mom, where were you last night?"

"I was having a couple of drinks with friends," she said.

I sat across from her and tried to tell her everything that had happened. As my excitement grew, my voice raised until she would remind me to lower the volume.

I mean, I told her everything. About what we saw, what we heard over the officer's radios. About my highly eventful ride home. Everything!

"Lonnie." My mom always sounded exasperated with me. I guess I bothered her too much. It became her "Lonnie" voice. Any time she was talking to me, she sounded tired. "Lonnie. I'm sure it was your imagination. You know how you are. Besides, the sun was in your eyes. You couldn't see anything. And then it was too dark. Don't talk about it anymore, to anyone. It just makes you sound silly. Now would you be a dear and pour me some more coffee?"

There was no point in trying to change her mind. Even though the sun was at my back, I clearly saw Bigfoot running across the street. Even though I'd had a close-up and personal meeting with the Bigfoot, my mother had decided I had imagined the whole thing.

In the fifty years since that summer day, I've seen the look people get when I try to tell them what I experienced. I might as well tell them an alien spacecraft beamed me up and stole my liver. I quit telling people.

That morning, after refilling my mom's coffee cup, I got on my bike and rode to the lumber yard. I tried to determine precisely where it came out on one side of the street, and where it went into the warehouse on the other side of the road. In my exploration, I realized, nobody worked in the warehouse. It was just a building where they kept lumber. I was hoping someone inside might have seen the Bigfoot, too. I looked around a bit but didn't see anything. Then, I walked back across to where the creature had first stepped out on the street. There were several large, wooden crates stacked near the road. I walked between two stacks and began looking around. I didn't see anything to confirm what Jeff and I had seen. As I started back out to my bike, disappointment enveloping me, I happened to glance up. I had been looking at the ground the whole time. And there it was, on the corner of an upper crate, caught in a splinter of the wood — a bunch of dark brown hair, or fur. At first, I began to freak out again, but then I thought, *That's it. Now I can prove it wasn't my imagination!*

I stuffed the fur in my pants pocket and rode home. I ran in the house, in all my excitement, forgetting to be quiet, and shouted, "Mom! I can prove it happened! Look what I found!"

I shoved it in her face. She wrinkled up her nose, grabbed my wrist, pushing my arm away from her face. "Oh, Good Lord, boy! I don't know why you insist on carrying on with this lie, but it ends here." She took the fur from my fingers and flushed all of my proof down the toilet.

"Lonnie," my mother began, "get in the car. We're going dumpster diving for cardboard boxes. We're moving to Arizona next week,"

Just like that, no discussion. My mother said we were leaving town, and she never let me see any of my friends again before we went. She even had the phone shut off. Once again, my mother was running away from something. That's what she did. Every couple of years, we'd move because she had ruined everything.

The day before we left town, Jeff came over. He asked me what my mother had said about the creature.

Mom called out from the next room, "Lonnie, tell your friend he has to go. You don't have time to play."

Jeff looked at me, then looked around at all the boxes and said, "Are you moving?"

I just nodded my head. He said, "But what about what we saw?"

My mom stuck her head around the corner of the wall and said, "Time to go. Have a nice day." She stood there watching us until Jeff finally just said goodbye and left.

As I grow old, I've begun to doubt my own story. If I ever bring it up, I say, "I have no idea what I saw that day, but when I was a kid, I was sure I saw Bigfoot." At this point, everyone laughs. I guess I'm hoping to find another like-minded person to share a similar experience. I'm sixty-two and have yet to meet anyone who has seen Bigfoot.

TERROR IN THE STREETS OF THE PHILIPPINES

Glenda Edlin Stevenson

We were heading in to do some shopping in Makati, the commercial district of Metro Manila, Philippines. This was our second year in the Philippines, where I was teaching school at Faith Academy for missionaries' children. My children also attended there.

Because of the incredible traffic of all kinds, human, motorcycle, bus, jeepney and cars, we found it difficult to go into the more modern part of the city to shop during the week. If anything was needed during the week, our maid, known as a "helper," shopped for food at the local open-air markets. I liked trying my hand bargaining at the *palengke*, Tagalog for "market," but my helper told me I didn't get good bargains, because I was American. This excursion was to the larger indoor grocery store (Walmart style) where prices were set, and there was a mall at the adjacent Green Hills shopping center, where we could find most anything else we needed.

As I was driving toward an intersection about halfway there, I noticed a military tank with three men dressed in army uniforms and armed with what looked like submachine guns, standing in the middle of the intersection. We had moved to the Philippines shortly after the coup that removed Marcos from office and replaced him with Mrs. Aquino as President of the country. I was well aware of several opposing military factions who still plagued the nation: NPA, the New People's Army, which was the communist group; MNLF, Moro National Liberation Front, the Muslim faction; and the *Nationalistica* Party, those still loyal to Marcos, who was then in exile.

There were several coup-attempts in the short two and one-half years we lived in the Philippines. Our children had coup-attempt days out of school rather than snow days like back home in the U.S. There always seemed to be an element of unrest, though the Filipino friends and neighbors we had were always friendly and helpful. Never did I encounter any hostility, so this was something entirely new for me. As we approached the armed intersection, my mind raced in a million directions. Should we turn around? What was going to happen to us? I was especially concerned, since my two girls were in the car with me.

There really was no place to turn around until we reached the intersection, since there was a concrete median in the road we were on, Ortigas Highway. As expected, the military men motioned us to stop. One of the men asked us to step out while they searched the car. Then, I was instructed to open the trunk, which, of course, I did. They searched it and then said we could proceed. Still shaking in my sandals, we proceeded to the shopping mall. I guess I was in shock and didn't know what else to do.

On Monday at school, I finally learned the reason for the military roadblock. The Philippine Minister of the Interior was missing, presumed kidnapped, along with his two bodyguards, so the roadblock was meant to find him. Unfortunately, all three men were found dead out near the back entrance to Faith Academy, Monday morning. Was this the only time we were in grave danger while living in the Philippines?

As far as I was aware, other than the coup-attempts which were further away distance-wise, this was the only time we seemed directly in harm's way. During the coup attempts, the school had a grapevine method of contacting students and teachers. The message was passed forward household to household. Each of us was assigned the next person on the list to contact. Not everyone had a land phone, and this was pre-cell-phone days. At those times, we were warned to stay home and inside until further notice. Otherwise, we were warned to be prudent at all times.

I remember clearly, as I breathed a sigh of relief while we drove on that day, how grateful I was that people back home in the U.S. had promised to pray for us while we were on this short-term mission trip. Never had I been more aware of the need to pray for missionaries than I was then. And I thought, we all should be praying for each other all the time. We never know what someone is facing at any given time.

Maybe I was calmer, because I was sure this was God's plan for me to be in the Philippines as a teacher at this time. Knowing you are in God's plan and being covered by God's people with prayer made facing this scary moment possible for me, while this is no guarantee that evil will not befall us. The only people I know personally who have been kidnapped, raped, murdered by terrorists, or robbed at gunpoint in a home invasion are missionaries whom I knew in the Philippines. Nevertheless, God promises to be with us to the end, so we still trust Him in the scary moments. In the familiar Psalm 23, King David wrote, "Even when I walk through the dark valley of death, I will not be afraid, for you are close beside me." God's presence is what makes the real difference in facing the scariest of times.

A GHOST STORY

By Rosemarie Sabel Durgin

When I was young, Mother and I lived in a small apartment subleased from the owner of the house. The house was on a street with a lot of little bungalows. There were kids living in all the houses, and we all played together after school. Our next-door neighbor was the town's cemetery. We girls loved to play in there.

The place was safe, no traffic to watch out for. We played hide and seek most days, and in winter, we would build snowmen and had snowball fights, made snow angels. We could hide amongst the tall shrubs and behind the gravestones, since we were all still quite small, pre-teenagers. Our mothers, too, liked for us to be nearby and out of harm's way. So, we played in the graveyard. At other times, we would go and look at some of the very old monuments and would imagine the lives of the people that had once lived in our town. The names were always so inspiring, like Charlotte Amalia Henrietta Therese von Hohenstaufen Ritter.

"Oh my gosh," we would gush, "that was a princess. A princess lived in our town. Was there once a castle here? Or did she just live in an ordinary house?"

"When did she live here?" we all wondered, and one of us would try to decipher the dates from the weathered stone. 1571 to 1643. Irene or Helga, were finally able to make it out.

"She was as old as my mother is now when she died," Renate would exclaim and become quiet, worried she might lose her mother any second now.

We all would move throughout the cemetery to search for her husband and children. If we found anyone with the matching name and matching time frame, then our imaginations would conjure up all kinds of stories about their lives. Yes, we girls had lots of fun playing and inventing stories about the inhabitants of the yard.

Then, one day the local boys challenged us. "Come out and play with us after dark." We did not want to. It was just too scary. We hid behind our mother's edict to be inside when night came. The boys, our brothers, knew better. They knew how to sneak out of the house, unseen by our parents, though they had been caught many a time outside, when they should have been inside.

On a late fall day, the boys had teased us enough, and we girls finally had our courage up and would meet the guys at midnight at the cemetery. Night fell at that time of the year around six o'clock in the evening, and we had decided not to leave before our mothers were asleep. The bathroom windows in several homes had been unlocked earlier in the day to make our escapes possible and quiet.

That particular night, like so many others in late fall, had fog wafting in over the meadows and up the hill even before it was totally dark. When we finally all assembled at the cemetery gate, it was so foggy, you barely could see the hand in front of your eyes or the person standing next to you. We girls shivered but tried not to show our fear. We were done with being called scaredy cat or sissy.

By popular vote, Horst, my friend Helga's brother, was elected to search for us, and we girls scattered about the graveyard as he counted to ten. Then, we had better be hiding. We did all find wonderful places to conceal ourselves. We knew which were the best places. Horst kept calling for us that he could not find us and had stumbled across several graves in his attempt to root us out. Shortly after that, I saw something semi-solid floating through the fog. What was that? I had no inkling. Then, Erika screamed.

"Oh, geez, it's a ghost. I am getting out of here."

The rest of us remained, a bit more cautious now. We did not want to be found by the ghost.

Horst too acted like he was scared and called to his sister to come on out and go home with him.

No, Helga did not believe in ghosts, and so she stayed put. So did Erika. I certainly was not going to leave and let the boys win; Renate, too, was with me, and so were Susie and Anneliese. The six of us stayed hidden, telling Horst to look for us. But our voices did not carry in the dense fog, and when they heard something, it was muffled.

Things got worse. Pretty soon, not just one ghost was floating about; several came along, and then they started whispering, telling us that we were disruptive and disrespectful.

Another voice was moaning, "Get off my head! You are hurting me." Another was laughing hysterically. We were getting chills running down our backs. A voice was complaining that we should let them rest in peace. They had earned their rest, after a hard life of toil.

Finally, we girls could not take it anymore. We ran out of the cemetery screaming in fright, to the complete amusement of the boys, as they removed the white sheets they had borrowed from the linen closets at home. We girls had the last laugh, though, because we won the game. Horst had not been able to find even one of us. We never let the boys forget that and would be sure to recall the incident, when they tried to portray us as sissies once again.

THE GREEN GODDESS

Andrea Foster

Cybill heard the door of the Green Goddess Floral shop swing open with a squeak and a tinkle of the bell.

"Sue Ann, could you get that, please?" Cybill was sitting in the office, staring at a computer screen, trying to decide what new, exotic flower she should bring into the shop this week. Should she consider a protea, just for something different? Or a new kind of lily or orchid? Cybill scrolled over the computer screen with her mouse, back and forth, back and forth, unable to decide.

"Yes, ma'am!" Sue Ann called back, and then, "How may I help you ladies today?"

A breathy, high-pitched Southern drawl replied excitedly, "Yes, we're here to pick my wedding flowers!"

Cybill smiled at the words. She loved putting together wedding arrangements, such a happy occasion! She sighed and continued to scroll down the pictures of the flowers, keeping one ear towards the conversation in case she needed to order something special.

"Now, Lydia, calm down. Let's talk to the

lady. The problem we have is that the wedding is rather short notice," said a slower, more mature sounding feminine voice.

"Pink! I want everything pink!" the younger voice exclaimed. "Mama, I don't care as long as they are PINK!" She raised the pitch of her voice on the word, "pink".

"Well, ladies, we have plenty of pink blossoms to choose from. How soon do you need the floral arrangements? Do you need a bouquet also?" Sue Ann was practical.

Now, Cybill was really listening in, wondering if she'd have to order something special."

"RROOOSSSES!" crooned the young voice, Lydia apparently. "I want pink ROOOSEES!" Here, her voice lowered and rolled the word out of her mouth. Then, the sound peaked again, "And I want them ALL to SMELL DIVINE!"

The more mature voice answered Sue Ann, "We need them two weeks from Saturday. We'll need a floral bouquet for the wedding, two large arrangements for either side of the altar, and small floral bouquets for twelve table decorations. They need to be short enough so the guests can see each other, but large enough to make a statement. Can that be done by then?"

"Yes, I am sure we can handle that." Sue Ann

knew they had done last minute events like this many times; they just called in reinforcements, and everybody scrambled to make it happen. "May I ask who the lucky groom is?" Sue Ann knew to make conversation, to make the bride-to-be feel special.

The younger voice chirped happily, "Mr. John Attis of Philadelphia! My fiancé! Ooh, Mama, look at these! But they don't smell!" She wrinkled her nose. "Why don't they smell?"

Cybill had been contentedly continuing to scroll through the PINK roses, mentally calculating an order, but suddenly her face became hot, and her eyes bulged at the screen. Her stomach dropped. She felt like she had just fallen off a roller coaster. She scooched her chair out and quickly breezed onto the shop floor, fussing with her hair to try to hide that she was trying to become emotionless. She pasted a smile on and asked in an extra-gushy voice, "Who did you say was your fiancé? Mr. John Attis, did you say?"

"Oh, yes, he is a doll!" said the young blonde with a hightop ponytail, leaning on the counter, with a fresh pink rose stuck up her nostrils. "Now, this one smells good! OOP!" She dropped it, and pulled her hand away, having pricked herself with a thorn.

Sue Ann commented, "The thornless roses are engineered to be safe to handle, but unfortunately, they don't smell at all. The genuine roses will always have thorns, so you have to be careful, but they smell great. We can have the thorns removed from your bouquet."

"Ah, yes, but she said she wants her flowers to be real and emit a powerful aroma, so surely she can endure a *prick* for her special day." Cybill was now especially focused. Her eyes had turned to slits, and her smile had gone flat. She was serious business now. "When did you say the wedding was?"

"Two weeks from Saturday," answered Lydia's mother, looking and fingering some baskets filled with different hues of roses. "The 14th." She was not looking at Cybill at all.

"Yes," answered Cybill, catching her breath and feeling pressure build in her chest. "We can make this happen. Sue Ann, please take their order. Whatever they want. We will give them a day they will never forget. Give them a 25% off discount. We will add some free vines and heart shaped runners. Our gift for the happy occasion." Cybill turned on her heel and left the room.

"Oh, goody!" exclaimed the young blonde, pony-tail bouncing.

"Why, thank you," added the mother. "Now, Lydia, let's get down to business, and choose, so these nice people can place our order."

"Now how about a very special *boutonniere* for my special man?" asked Cybill, with a sharp smile and squint. "I mean, *your* special man."

"Oh, I can't wait!!" exclaimed the blondie.

"Neither can I," answered Cybill under her breath, imagining the perfect herbal concoctions she would use to incite her revenge.

BRIAN'S HAUNTED HOUSE

By A. Tuna Dobbins

Brian moved to town just recently and isn't sure how long he's going to stay, so he's looking for a house to rent. He doesn't want to spend the money the real estate agents are asking for on the newer homes in the town, and most of the older homes are in bad neighborhoods or, at least, ones that he doesn't want to live in. After a couple of weeks of looking at homes that the agents have on their books and not finding one he likes, he decides to drive around the town to see if someone has any "For Rent" or "For Lease" signs out front. Before long, he spots a "For Lease" sign in front of an older home on the outskirts of town. He parks his car on the street and takes a look around. The home has an acre or more of land around it and an old picket fence that needs some work. The house looks pretty good, even though it needs fresh paint.

Brian pulls into the driveway that leads to a detached garage, which was probably a barn at some time in the past. He gets out and walks to the front door. The house looks empty. There is an old door knocker on the center of the front door and no sign of a doorbell. Brian uses the knocker and knocks several times. There is no response.

He peers inside and sees an empty front room. Dusty but nice. The walls look like they were painted recently, and the hard wood floors are shiny. Brian pulls out his cell phone and calls the number on the sign. After a few rings, a woman answers.

"Hello."

"Hi, I'm looking at the old house on Manor Lane. The 'For Lease' sign out front has this phone number. Are you the person interested in renting it?"

"You must be new in town."

"Yes. How did you know?"

"I've had that sign up on that house for over a year now, and you're the first person to call me."

"Is there something wrong with the house?"

"No. No. The house is in great shape for its age. The appliances were updated about two years ago, and the wiring brought up to code. Would you like to look at it?"

"Yes. When can you be here?"

"I can be there in fifteen minutes."

"Thanks. I'll take a look at the property in the meantime."

Brian walks around the house and peers in every window. The house appears to be completely empty, except for a single picture hanging over the fireplace.

Brian makes a complete circle around the house and is about to reach the front porch again, when a car pulls up behind his car. A middle-aged woman gets out.

"You must be the man I talked to earlier." The woman sticks out her hand.

"I'm Samantha."

"Hi, Samantha. I'm Brian. Tell me more about the house."

"Gladly. Let's go in."

Samantha leads Brian up the walk to the front porch and unlocks the door.

"The house was built in 1913. There are two bedrooms and one bathroom. It belonged to my great-grandparents. After they passed on, I had it upgraded – new wiring, new appliances, central heat and air, paint, well, basically everything inside."

Brian follows Samantha around the house, and it is very nice inside as she said it would be. Since it is completely empty, there is a slight echo to everything they say.

After walking around the property again with Samantha, Brian says, "I'll take it."

"Let's go back to my house, and I'll take care of the paperwork."

Brian follows Samantha to her home, where he provides all his personal information. Samantha accepts a check from Brian for the deposit and first month's rent.

"I'll check your references, then get back to you."

"Okay. I'd like to move in before the end of the month," Brian advises her.

"I'm sure that will not be a problem."

A few days later, Samantha calls Brian to let him know that he can have the house. They agree to meet at the house for one last look and to exchange the key. Brian calls a rental company, as he'll need some bedroom, living room and dining room furniture.

After walking through the house one more time, Samantha hands him the keys and heads for the front door. As she steps out on to the porch, she looks back at Brian.

"Oh, one more thing. That picture above the fireplace is my great-grandmother. She loved this house and specified in her will that her picture should remain above the fireplace, so I'd like you to promise me to never touch that picture and never take it down."

"Okay, but why?"

"Trust me on this. It would be better for

everyone if that picture stays exactly where it is."

Brian nods, and Samantha walks out to her car.

A couple of days later, the rental agency delivers a dining table with two chairs, a couch, a coffee table, a flat screen TV, and a table for it to stand on, a bed and a dresser. Brian is ready to move in. He fills the refrigerator and pantry with food, then orders a pizza for his first meal in his "new" house. He's too tired to cook and not interested in eating out like he has for the previous few weeks. There are only three TV channels available, since he hasn't ordered a cable or satellite system yet.

Brian kicks back on the couch with a cold beer and catches a couple of hours of what the local TV stations have to offer. The picture above the fireplace appears to be staring at him. When the picture was taken, the old woman was looking directly at the camera, so wherever he is in the living room, the woman is staring at him. He looks around the living room at the bare walls and wonders what sort of pictures the old lady would have hung when she lived in the house.

Time for bed. Brian gets off the couch and has to walk by the fireplace on his way to the bedroom. He waves his hand at the old woman in the picture and says, "Good night." As he looks away from the picture, he hears a soft voice say, "Good night."

Brian stops and looks around. There's no one but him in the living room. *This old house still has an echo.*

Over the next week or so, Brian pays little attention to the picture. Then one night, he stops in front of the fireplace and looks at the picture for several seconds. *I wonder what the big deal is with the picture.* Standing this close to it, it looks a little crooked. He reaches up and touches the frame to straighten it. When his fingers touch the picture, he feels a little tingle in his fingertips. Brian takes his hand off the picture, and the tingle stops. *Wow.*

He reaches up to the picture again and gives it a little move to the left to make it square with the fireplace. Not much of a move, but enough to realize that when the house was painted, the painter painted around the picture, not behind it. *I'll take care of that later.*

After going to bed, Brian hears a creak and sits up in the bed. He listens for several minutes without hearing another sound. During the night, he is awakened twice more by creaking noises in the house. After the second time, he gets up and takes a look through the house. He's the only one there. As he's heading back to his bedroom, he notices that the picture is crooked again and completely covering the old paint on the wall. *Must be the wind.*

"Hello."

"Samantha, this is Brian, your renter."

"Yes, Brian. What can I do for you?"

"Do you still have any of the paint used to paint the living room walls?"

"I think so, why?"

"The painter didn't paint behind your great-grandmother's picture, so I thought I'd take care of that for you."

Gasp. "Did you move her picture?"

"Yeah. It was a little crooked, so I tweaked it. That's when I noticed that the painter did not paint behind it."

"Did anything unusual happen after you moved the picture?"

"No, not really. I felt a little tingle when I touched it but only for a second."

"That's all?"

"Yeah, why?"

"Oh, no reason. Just wondering."

"The funny thing is that the picture was back in place this morning."

"Back in place?"

"Yeah. I didn't move it very much, so the wind last night must have shaken the house a little and moved it back to where it was."

"What wind? Last night wasn't windy."

"It must have been windy out at the old house, because I heard the house creak a few times last night."

Oh no! "Brian, I'll check on that paint for you, but I really don't think you need to paint behind the picture. It's not necessary, and you can always tell exactly where the painting should be if you every move it again."

She's being weird.

"If you say so. If you find the paint, let me know and we'll go from there."

"Okay. Have a great day."

Later that day, Brian is standing at the fireplace and looking at the picture. It's still a little crooked, but it completely hides the old paint. Brian leans against the wall to look behind the picture. *Is there something hiding back there that Samantha doesn't want me to find?*

The picture is hung tightly against the wall with almost no gap to look into. Brian carefully pulls the bottom of the picture away from the wall and sees nothing behind it but bare wall. His fingertips tingle a little again. Brian puts the picture back against the wall and makes sure it completely covers the old paint. He takes a deep breath and lets it out. He hears a faint echo of this deep breath and looks around. *There's still an echo in here.*

After going to bed, he hears the house creak again. Just once. The next morning, he looks at the picture. It appears to be exactly where he put it yesterday. Before leaving the house for work, he takes a pencil and puts a mark on either side of the picture. Then, he very slightly moves the picture. His fingertips tingle again.

Brian steps back and looks at his hands, then at the picture. For a second, he thinks the eyes of the old woman are glaring at him. Then, the glare fades.

When Brian returns to the house after work, he checks the picture, and it is hung evenly between the pencil markings, as it was before he moved it. *That's really weird! Something is shaking the house just enough to make the picture return to its original place after I move it.*

"Hello."

"Samantha, Brian again. I've got another question for you about the house."

What has he done now? "What do you need to know?"

"How do I get into the attic? I've looked around for a door or something that opens into the attic, but I'm not finding one."

"Oh. Let me think." Samantha pauses for several seconds, then says, "I don't think there is any access to the attic. At least, I can't remember any."

He'd better not find a way into the attic!

"Okay. Thanks."

I've never seen a house without access to the attic. There's got to be one somewhere.

A couple of days later, Brian is looking in the old garage and finds an old wooden ladder. The rungs are a little loose, but Brian finds some nails and a hammer. He drives new nails into the rungs to tighten them up. Next, he takes the ladder to the closet in his bedroom and climbs high enough to reach the ceiling and give it a push up. It doesn't budge.

The second bedroom closet is next. This bedroom is still completely empty, and noises echo a little here. After leaning the ladder against the back wall of the closet, Brian climbs up and pushes up on its ceiling. It moves. Brian pushes the false ceiling up and slides it sideways. He climbs a little higher and sticks his head up in the attic. It's pitch black, and Brian can only see a few feet in any direction. What he sees is nothing, except ceiling joists and rafters. *I need a flashlight. Duh!*

Brian climbs back down, leaving the ladder in place and the ceiling panel out of place.

The next day, Brian has a new flashlight, and he climbs the ladder again. With the flashlight, Brian can see all across the attic from the closet hatch. On the far side of the attic is a small trunk. A very old small trunk. There's no room to stand up in the attic, so Brian crawls across the attic from joist to joist. He drags the trunk back to the closet hatch, then climbs part way down the ladder. The trunk just barely fits through the hatch. The trunk feels heavy, so there must be something inside it.

The only problem is that it is locked. The old hasp requires a skeleton key to unlock it. *Do I ask Samantha for the key or just pry it open?*

Brian decides to sleep on it.

The next day, Brian decides to pry it open. He has the claw hammer from the garage, after all. When he gets home, he gets the old hammer from the garage, then walks inside. The old woman in the picture appears to be glaring at him again, but only for a split second. Brian pauses in the living room and looks at the picture for several more seconds before heading to the second bedroom.

When he slips the claws of the hammer between the hasp and the trunk, his hands tingle. Brian lets go of the hammer and looks at his hands. They stop tingling. *Is this just me, or is something trying to tell me something?* He grabs the hammer again and with one quick pull, pops the hasp up and out of the lock. There is a loud creak. Brian looks up, then all around. He's the only one in the room.

Brian releases the other two latches on the trunk and lifts the lid. All he finds in the trunk are some canning jars wrapped with old newspaper and rags. As he removes the first jar and unwraps it, there is another loud creak in the house. Brian pauses to listen, but all is quiet again. He wipes the dust off the top of the jar, and there is a name written on it – Jacob.

There are five more jars in the trunk, and all have names on them. The jars appear to be partly filled with sand or ash. As Brian works up the nerve to open one of the jars, there is another creak in the house. Brian has heard the house creak enough times to not let it bother him. This time, he should have looked around.

As he starts to turn the lid on the jar, there is a sharp pain in his chest. He looks down and sees the tip of a blade sticking out of his chest. The blade is quickly removed, and Brian falls over on his side. Samantha is standing over him with a sword in her hands.

That night, a fire is built in the fireplace even though it is not cold outside. Later, the trunk is returned to the attic with a new jar inside. This jar is labeled "Brian." The false ceiling in the second bedroom closet is glued in place. The ladder and hammer are returned to the garage. The "For Lease" sign is again standing in front of the old house.

ABOUT OUR AUTHORS

Bruce Baker taught English Literature and Writing to middle school students, primarily Hispanic, first and second generation immigrants, after retiring from a career in information systems. An accomplished photographer, he has won awards for his work at the State Fair of Oklahoma. He has published op-ed pieces in the *Daily Oklahoman* as well as short stories in a local church publication. His first major work, *Accidental Refugee,* is complete and ready for publication. Mr. Baker lives with his wife Deborah in Oklahoma City.

Judy Winchester-Beitia is a newly budding writer venturing into the genres of romance and mystery. She is a mother with many talents and not only runs a landscaping business but also an art photography studio. She is a mother of three who lives in Edmond with her husband, two daughters, and two big dogs, as well as thousands of faerie-sprites in her gardens.

Judy K. Bishop writes inspirational children's books, poetry, short stories and essays. She has a book of poetry called *Poetry Pathway,* and her new novel is *Destiny Called my Name.* Before becoming a member of Oklahoma City Writers, Inc., Romance

Writers of America, Oklahoma Writers Federation, and Creative Quills, she lived in Hawaii for almost twenty years. She resides in Choctaw, OK.

Garrett Clifton is a gifted horror writer and performance artist from Oklahoma City. He is well known not only for his suspenseful writing and a "Choose Your Own Adventure" style spooky story that he performed at an Our Glass Spooky Story Night, but also for his vivid reading and character portrayals. His new book is *Horror at the Water's Edge.*

Alton "Tuna" Dobbins retired from the Air Force in 1996 with over 2000 hours in single seat attack jets. He then worked for the Federal Aviation Administration as a technical writer until retiring in 2015. Tuna is the author of four fiction novels: *Crossbow Revenge, Alice Was Not Her Name, Antiques To Die For,* and *Hyperdeath,* all action-packed murder mysteries. Tuna is a fan of fast cars and participates in shows and open road racing in his Corvette. He has an autobiography titled *Tuna, Uncanned* and resides in Mustang, OK with his wife Susan.

Rosemarie Sabel Durgin was born just before WWII in Germany. She came to America in 1963 and is the mother of four and grandmother of ten. She is retired, except for writing full time! She currently has four books: *Kinder Castle, Mail Order Bride, Journey to Freedom and Independence,* and *Going Green,* with a number of others in the works! She is a member of Romance Writers of America and Creative Quills. Rose also does some editing and is a book-formatting expert. Besides writing, Rosemarie enjoys traveling, reading, needlework, wildlife and photography. Rosemarie lives in El Reno, Oklahoma, with a menagerie of cats and dogs.

Debbie Fogle enjoys life to the fullest in her world of make believe! A member of Creative Quills writing group of El Reno, Oklahoma, she is published in all of their anthologies. She is a former member of Romance Writers of America and was a judge of the Young Adult category for OKRWA – NRCA. She has been active in various writers' clubs, including the California Writer's Club as a 2019-2020 category Judge for Scholastic Art & Writing Contest for Short Story with Writers of Kern of the California Writer's Club. Her published novels include: *All of Us in Darkness, Passenger with the Airbag Off, And Another Thing... A Collection of Short Stories, A Candy Cane Christmas, Chain of Events, Kissing it All Goodbye,* and *Mr. & Mrs. V- An Everlasting Love.* She lives in

Oklahoma with her pen and paper.

Andrea Foster is an editor and author who has been in the book business since 1977. She currently coaches the Academic Team at Redlands Community College, teaches Creative Writing at the Carnegie Library in El Reno, and how to Write Publish & Market Your Book at the Canadian Valley Technology Center, CVTech. She is a former adjunct instructor for Redlands Community College in Writing, Composition and Argument. A former Op Ed writer for various newspapers in Connecticut, she also did research and investigative reporting on such diverse subjects as government involvement in the arts, nuclear power plants, and toxic waste. She has written a variety of books on a diverse number of subjects. She lives in Kingfisher with her kitty cats and large personal library.

Melonie B. Hylan, who writes from her home in Norman, Oklahoma, is a retired professor of English and author of an amateur detective series that draws on her Oklahoma background. Melonie grew up in Oklahoma and received her BA, MA, and PhD in English from the University of Oklahoma. Her first novel is *Ashes, Ashes. . .* which introduces a sixty-eight-year-old retiree-turned-sleuth. In her second novel, *Pitchforks and Pocketknives*, the same sleuth investigates an unsolved, small-town mystery from 1964. When Melonie is not writing, studying Spanish, trying out vegetarian recipes, or gardening, she teaches yoga and looks for opportunities to speak out as an uppity woman.

Lynn Dell Jones was born in New Orleans, Louisiana, and raised in Oklahoma. She started her career in computer technology 10 years before the internet was even invented. With awards and recognition from that industry, she now is embarking on a writing career with the same tenacity and longevity. Her first published work was a short story in the Creative Quills' short story anthology *Christmas Treasures: From Our Past to Your Present*. She continues to work on her other literary works that include her memoirs and tales of supernatural Welsh fiction. She is a prominent member of the LGBTQ community as a member and diversity advocate. Coincidentally, she resides in Jones, Oklahoma, where she lives with her one-eyed cat.

Kristina Lee has been writing all her life. She has an undergraduate degree in psychology and a master's degree in counseling. A member of Creative Quills, she also paints, writes poetry and short stories. Her first novel *Faerborne Scorn* is due to be available to the public soon. She lives in Midwest City, Oklahoma with her husband who is in the military, their child, and two cats.

Bernadette Lowe, a farmer's daughter, grew up on a dairy farm filled with laughter and fun In recent years, she has written a short book on how to buy a car for next to nothing, and she has completed an intensive family history, entitled *Mosman: An Illustrious Family*, which includes a wealth of general historical knowledge, due to become its own volume soon. She is now a grandmother who loves writing stories for her granddaughter and lives in Oklahoma City, OK.

JoJo Maize is a veteran of the United States Air Force and military sexual assault survivor. She is on a mission to bring awareness to sexual assault in the military. Ms. Maize is currently a member of a writing group in El Reno, Oklahoma, Creative Quills. She and her husband of 40+ years have lived in Yukon, Oklahoma since 1983. They enjoy traveling the highways and by-ways of the United States.

Julie Marquardt is a haiku poet extraordinaire, and author of young adult stories. After joining the

Creative Quills writing group in 2015, she rediscovered her love of writing. Her first young adult novel, *Brigantina's Journey* features a sea-loving young lady from the 1800's who finds herself mixed up with pirates and other adventures. Julie also has short stories published in *Alternate Perspectives, Tales and Trails: A Western Odyssey,* and *Christmas Treasures: From our Past to Your Present.* She lives in Oklahoma with two dogs and a cat and is currently working on Brigantina's continuing escapades.

Les McDermott has written two books, *The Diner* and *Prose Quotes and Short Stories* as well as three short stories in Creative Quills' short story anthologies *Christmas Treasures: From Our Past to Your Present* and *Murder Mystery and Mayhem.* Les loves writing fiction and using his imagination.

Glenda Edlin Stevenson, having retired from teaching math/science classes and from accounting at OSBI, now has more time for her creative side of writing. She began producing her own newsletter while teaching missionaries' children in the Philippines. Upon returning to the United States, Glenda soon began journaling to deal with reverse culture shock, career change and depression. Her journaling expanded as she trained to become a

Biblical counselor at Scope Ministries International. As a trainee at Scope, she continued writing an inspirational newsletter called "Discoveries." Her passion is discipleship. She lives in Oklahoma City near her two daughters and two young grandsons who provide a lot of material for her writing. She is a member of Wordwrights Christian Writers Group and Creative Quills. She won 2nd place for her Christmas prose piece "A Long-Awaited Gift" with Wordwrights in 2019. Her new book is *More Than a Diary: Journaling to Be Transformed* by Glenda Edlin Stevenson.

F. A. Walker is a budding writer and former businessman and Marine pilot from Havelock, North Carolina. His interests include history and jazz music. He is currently writing a family memoir that looks at his ancestral heritage through the lens of both personal stories and American history.

OTHER BOOKS BY OUR AUTHORS

Poetry Pathways by Judy K. Bishop

Destiny Called my Name by Judy K. Bishop

Horror at the Water's Edge by Garrett Clifton

Crossbow Revenge by A. "Tuna" Dobbins

Alice Was Not Her Name by A. "Tuna" Dobbins

Antiques to Die For by A. "Tuna" Dobbins

Tuna, Uncanned by A. "Tuna" Dobbins

Hyperdeath by A. "Tuna" Dobbins

Going Green by Rosemarie Sabel Durgin

Kinder Castle by Rosemarie Sabel Durgin

Mail Order Bride by Rosemarie Sabel Durgin

Journey to Freedom and Independence by Rosemarie Sabel Durgin

The Quiet War by Rosemarie Sabel Durgin

A Candy Cane Christmas by Debbie Fogle

All of Us in Darkness by Debbie Fogle

And Another Thing: A Collection of Short Stories by Debbie Fogle

Chain of Events by Debbie Fogle

Happiness is Hard to Find by Debbie Fogle

Kissing It All Good-bye by Debbie Fogle

Passenger with the Airbag Off by Debbie Fogle

Mr. and Mrs. V by Debbie Fogle

Helena and the Haunted Hospital by Andrea Foster

The Laws of Love by Andrea Foster

Zodiac Problems and Solutions by Andrea Foster

The Hidden Transition by Lynn Dell Jones

Mosman: An Illustrious Family by Bernadette Lowe

Mama's Dark Secrets: Unmasking Evil by JoJo Maize

Brigantina's Journey by Julie Marquardt

The Diner by Les McDermott

Prose Quotes and Short Stories by Les McDermott

More Than a Diary: Journaling to Be Transformed by Glenda Edlin Stevenson

OTHER BOOKS BY CREATIVE QUILLS WRITING GROUP

Alternate Perspectives

Tales and Trails: A Western Odyssey

The Way We Were: Adventures in Childhood

Christmas Treasures: From our Past to Your Present

OUR WEBSITES

http://www.creativequills.com

http://www.okwriters.com

http://www.meetup.com/CreativeQuills/

http://www.writeok.com

http://www.patreon.com/CreativeQuills

http://www.facebook.com/CreativeQuills

Creative Quills Publishing Group always seeks to make our books better, and errors are inevitable, as our mind plays tricks on us, no matter how many people beta-read our books. If you find punctuation or spelling errors in this book, please write to booklady@creativequills.com and inform us of the error. If we find you're right, (and the error was not intentional) you get another one of our books FREE! Thank you for reading and helping!

Made in the USA
Columbia, SC
23 October 2020